When the cars had disappeared around the bend of the road in front of Zig-Zag, Betty took Reuben's key from her bag and unlocked the door again.

She stood beside the reception desk and planned how she would search the floor, office by office. For a moment, Betty relaxed. It was probably all a fool's errand she'd come on.

Suddenly Betty froze.

One of the lights on the telephone console came on. Someone was making a call from somewhere in the Zig-Zag building. . . .

Also by Joyce Christmas
Published by Fawcett Books:

Lady Margaret Priam series

A FÊTE WORSE THAN DEATH
SUDDENLY IN HER SORBET
SIMPLY TO DIE FOR
A STUNNING WAY TO DIE
FRIEND OR FAUX
IT'S HER FUNERAL

THIS
BUSINESS
IS MURDER

Joyce Christmas

FAWCETT GOLD MEDAL • NEW YORK

A Fawcett Gold Medal Book
Published by Ballantine Books
Copyright © 1993 by Joyce Christmas

All rights reserved under International and Pan-American Copyright Conventions. Published in the United States of America by Ballantine Books, a division of Random House, Inc., New York, and simultaneously in Canada by Random House of Canada Limited, Toronto.

Library of Congress Catalog Card Number: 93-90191

ISBN 0-449-14800-9

Manufactured in the United States of America

First Edition: August 1993

"For the glory"
of my golden friends,
Naomi and Don Shuey

CHAPTER 1

THEY DIDN'T give Betty Trenka a gold watch when she retired from Edwards & Son after thirty-seven years on the job. They gave her a clock for a mantelpiece she didn't have. It was very nice, very expensive. Sid Edwards Jr.'s wife had excellent taste, as she'd be the first to tell you.

Betty would later say that she bought the little house in East Moulton, Connecticut, with some of the money Sid Senior had seen she'd gotten, just to have a place to put that damned clock.

A discreet little gold plaque affixed under the face read BETTY TRENKA, with the dates she'd worked at Edwards & Son, all but the last two years with Sid Edwards, Sr., working her way up from typist to office manager, to friend and even adviser. The clock made it sound as though she'd died the day she walked out of the office for the last time.

Well, Betty might be dead, but Elizabeth Anne Trenka was alive and well and living on a woodsy acre of land in a five-room shingle house that was quite a bit older than she. There were three aggressively healthy blue spruces in front and a neglected garden in back. And yes, it had a fireplace with a mantel.

Someone had asked her why East Moulton. She supposed it reminded her of the town where she'd grown up, but what she told her questioner was that she wanted a complete change from the pleasant Hartford suburb where she'd lived for years.

In the living room Betty glared at the hopeless piles of cartons that had been just sitting there for three days while

1

she got up the enthusiasm to unpack. She liked order, so she'd been careful to label each carton with its contents, but the prospect of opening the boxes up and finding a place for everything was not appealing. She could keep an office full of chattering girls and blustering executives running so smoothly they didn't know what had hit them. She could keep herself decently dressed and well enough fed, but in her sixty-three years she had not become a domestic person. The idea of attempting to be one at this late date was mildly appalling, but she wasn't ready to admit she'd made a mistake.

That's what really burned her up. She should be spending the next fifteen years or so continuing to do what she did best. Instead, she had rosebushes that needed attention. She'd have to buy one of those clipper things come spring.

Every time she thought about Sid Junior's decision to restructure the company after he took it over, she felt a rush of anger. Get rid of the high-priced senior employees like Betty and bring in a bevy of postteen beauties with less elevated salary requirements. She'd gone meekly, as far as the company was concerned: She hadn't sued for one thing, although she'd thought about it. She just wasn't happy. Sid Senior wasn't happy about the changes at the company either, but he was out in Arizona with his wife now, enjoying his "golden years."

Betty attacked the sealing tape on a carton of books. Golden, indeed. Sid Senior hadn't wanted to retire any more than she had, but at least he had his wife to pester the livelong day.

"Always look out for the guy who signs the checks," Sid Senior had told her when he retired. "And especially keep an eye on the one the money belongs to."

She hadn't heeded his advice: She'd forgotten that it had become Junior's money for all practical purposes.

Betty opened the box of books. She would force herself to arrange them in the empty bookcase the movers had placed against the wall. The books were mostly fiction: mysteries, some "serious" novels she'd liked and some she hadn't been able to finish; a few travel books about places she'd never had the time to visit; some histories and biographies. She certainly had the time now.

The phone ringing in her unsettled living room during the middle of a Friday morning startled her. The first thing that came to mind was that the telephone company had done its job right for once.

"Elizabeth Trenka," she said. She liked the sound of her name as it had appeared on her baptismal certificate, long before she became reliable, hardworking Betty.

"You don't know me, Miss . . . Mrs. . . . ? Ms. Trenka," a male voice said. "Jerry Preston, president of Zig-Zag Incorporated. We're over here in Hammond Center. I understand you can type. Know the alphabet? Word processing? Computers? You do know about writing business letters?"

The questions suggested to Betty a deep-seated insecurity based on unfortunate past experiences in an office. The voice sounded both young and nervous.

"Yes to all of those things," she said.

"And you're not young?" This was offered cautiously.

Probably a good bit older than you, sonny, she thought, but she said politely, "Age is relative. Maturity is measurable. Are you asking about my notice in the grocery store?"

She'd seen the community bulletin board on Wednesday when she'd gone into the small East Moulton Supermarket to buy mundane essentials she hadn't bothered to bring from her old apartment: instant coffee, milk, toilet paper, light bulbs. It was covered with handwritten notices about baby-sitting, kittens wanting homes, a car for sale, handymen available for outside work, expert sewing done in your own home. She'd stood for a long time looking at the bulletin board.

When she knew she'd be leaving Edwards & Son, she'd looked at the help-wanted ads in the Hartford paper. She could do just about anything in an office, but she didn't think she fit the image of an eager, self-starting "Gal/Guy Friday" the ads seemed to want.

There was her age, for one thing. And she guessed she

looked formidable and a bit eccentric to strangers, although she was formidable only when necessary and perfectly ordinary in other respects. She was quite tall for a woman. Her hands were large. She favored rather long skirts no matter what the current style. Her neighbor Cora Welles used to tell her that she had good legs and ought to show them off, but at her age she didn't think good legs mattered all that much. Her hair was thick and somewhat wiry. It was graying, but not entirely gray. She resisted the idea of coloring the gray away. Her face was not young, but people said she didn't look her age, whatever that meant. She had the usual wrinkles about her eyes, but they were nice eyes, although she'd always worn glasses that had gotten thicker with time. She was a hard worker with a lot of good years left.

After thinking about it overnight, she'd typed up a notice on her old portable: "New resident of East Moulton, recently retired, is seeking temporary employment, full- or part-time. Decades of experience. Typing, bookkeeping, general office work." She'd signed it Elizabeth Trenka and added the unfamiliar new telephone number attached to her new white cordless phone.

"Look," Jerry Preston said. "I need a girl for a few days. I mean, I need a *person* good in the office. I don't have time to train or explain. We're going to be shorthanded next week, Ms. . . . Elizabeth?" He seemed to feel he was talking to a stern old auntie.

"Betty," she said, resigned. "Just call me Betty."

"Yes, well. Betty." Betty was an ordinary name that suggested an ordinary person speaking respectfully to the boss. He could deal with a Betty. "My assistant, Denise, has to take a few days off for personal business, and the others can't . . . I wonder if you could come in for, say, three days at the beginning of the week? Correspondence is beginning to pile up, and my accounts receivable could use some help. It would only be temporary, you understand, but we'd pay you well. Nine to five-thirty."

"I'll be there on Monday at nine," Betty said. "Or earlier?"

"Eight-thirty would be great. I could show you around before the others come in." He sounded awfully young now. Then an afterthought: "You do have references?"

"I certainly do," she said. She must have spoken so firmly that he decided not to pursue it. In any case, she'd prefer not to bring Edwards & Son into this if she could avoid it. "Could I ask why you didn't go to a temp agency?"

"We didn't want an inexperienced kid out of high school," he said. "And I don't want somebody who's *really* an artist or *really* a potterymaker, or a housewife dying to get away from the kids for a few days, but when they run a temperature—" He stopped abruptly. "I shouldn't be saying that. I just want . . ."

"Three days of hard work, no questions being asked so none has to be answered."

"Give a shout when you come into the office. The door will be open." Young Jerry Preston, president of Zig-Zag Incorporated, sounded relieved to have found an old dame who could probably spell. "I'll be here. Our receptionist won't be anywhere near the front desk at eight-thirty on a Monday."

So, Betty decided, I could be an axe murderer or a drug dealer, but as long as I can turn on the copier without reading the instruction book, I'm welcome.

She'd forgotten to ask him exactly how well he paid or what Zig-Zag did. She did have a vague idea where Hammond Center was, but it didn't matter. She knew how to find things out. The prospect of having something to do in two days' time inspired her to plunge into the unpacking and bring some order into her new life.

CHAPTER 2

"It's a real quiet little town. I hope you won't find it too lonely out here."

Penny Saks, the irrepressibly cheerful young woman who was Betty's neighbor across a large unmowed field still bright with late wildflowers, appeared on the doorstep on Friday afternoon, eager to inspect Betty. At least she'd waited a couple of days after the movers had brought Betty's belongings from the old apartment near Hartford.

"This part of East Moulton was never built up," Penny said. "Greg says it probably won't ever be now. Greg's in insurance," she added hopefully. Betty had plenty of insurance, but she supposed she'd have to accept a professional call from Penny's husband to keep the neighborhood peaceful.

"Mr. Kelso across the street from you isn't well, so he doesn't go out too much," Penny reported as she surreptitiously examined Betty's furniture.

"I haven't seen him yet," Betty said. Edward Kelso's low stone house on the other side of Timberhill Road was half hidden behind a defensive wall of pines and maples.

"He doesn't visit around much," Penny said. "Isn't this pretty?" She was peering at Betty's retirement clock. "All those years at one company?"

"It was a parting gift," Betty said. "It's the thought that counts." Frankly, she'd rather have had the cash, under the circumstances.

"Alida Brill lives on the other side of you, down the hill. She's *always* off traveling, bless her, and she's not young."

Penny looked at Betty quickly, then back at the clock. Betty imagined she was kicking herself mentally—Betty was also certainly "not young."

"Then there are the people next to Alida. They say he drinks."

"Would you like coffee?" Betty asked. "I only have instant, I'm afraid. Or sherry?" That was about all she had in the house except for a couple of frozen dinners and a few things for sandwiches.

"Coffee would be great. Is there anything Greg and I can do to help you get settled?"

Although Betty refused aid at the moment, she had plans for Penny Saks. One of Betty's personal management strategies was to delegate to those who knew something she didn't. Penny was a good prospect for knowing which store at the big mall off the highway had the best buys.

"I could use your help getting new curtains for this room," Betty said as they sipped their coffee.

"Oh, sure! No problem. We could to it Monday."

"I can't. I'm working for a few days at a place called Zig-Zag Incorporated in Hammond Center."

"Aren't you amazing! Just retired and you're back to work."

"Temporarily. I seem to recall that Hammond Center isn't far."

"Straight through town along Main Street, then four or five miles more. There's not much there, the old village and a minimall. They've built an office park, but it hasn't been much of a success. That's what Greg says."

They were inspecting the windows when Betty noticed a trio of towheaded boys in the Sakses' front yard gleefully attacking one another with a variety of swords and missiles.

"Oh, gosh. It's my kids at it again! Whitey is impossible!" Penny headed for the front door. "Call if you need anything. Anytime." The sound of an exasperated mother hung on the air as she tore across the field separating the two houses. "Whitey! Stop it! I mean it!"

Perhaps, Betty thought, as the boys broke off their rampage, they are all called Whitey for the sake of convenience.

By the day's end Betty was tired and beginning to feel defeated by the chores the move necessitated. She'd started thinking about hiring one of those handymen to wash the windows on the outside, upstairs and down. She hated all this settling-in business. She hated the changes she'd been forced to accept.

She let down the stark, unfriendly venetian blinds in the living room. Through the trees she could see a light over the front door of Edward Kelso's house. The sight of it brought on a pang of loneliness. She wished she could think of something she needed so she could call Penny Saks. Someone to see, someone to talk to. Even the rambunctious Saks boys would be welcome. Then she had to laugh. Imagine her inviting a trio of blond demons in for cookies and milk, neither of which she had in the house.

During her years she'd lived alone, she had never been lonely. There had always been things to do, people to see. Cora and Dave Welles, her neighbors in the apartment complex, were always in and out for dinners and brunches and games of cards. Once a month or so her old friend, Eugene, drove down from Massachusetts for Sunday lunch and a movie in Hartford. She worked for political candidates, chosen by perceived ability rather than by party. She had her big open house every Christmas. Sometimes she visited her cousin Joe Trenka and his wife, Dorothy, in Pennsylvania. Once in a great while she went to Boston and saw her cousin Rita, a near contemporary on her mother's side of the family who had chosen to become a nun and serve the poor. Sister Rita had a perfectly innocent way of making Betty feel vaguely guilty about matters of faith and commitment, so she always sent her a hundred dollars at Christmas to use in her work. It didn't help much to ease the guilt.

And, of course, there was the office she'd been a part of for so many years, with its intricate patterns of competition, jealousies, and romances on top of all the work. That had certainly kept her well occupied. Thirty-seven years.

Although she'd lived alone for decades, she'd never been a lonely person.

"Let's face it, Elizabeth my friend," she said aloud. "You're feeling lonely now." Lonely. Old. Retired.

At least I'll ease into this retirement business with good grace, she promised herself firmly, but she knew she was lying about one thing: The Elizabeth Anne Trenka of her fantasy might be a model of good grace, but the real Betty Trenka was not. Betty was stubborn, opinionated, and capable of doing whatever she set her mind to.

She was damned if she was going to be either old or lonely for a long time to come. A little deafness in one ear and the bad knee that acted up now and then didn't make her old.

She'd work for a few days at Zig-Zag Incorporated and then she'd find a hobby, something she'd never before had time for. She'd take that trip. Maybe she'd take courses at the community college she knew was only a few miles away.

Betty looked around her.

First of all, she'd get this place into shape, invite the neighbors in. Edward Kelso, Penny and Greg Saks, the older traveling lady, and even the man who allegedly drank and his wife who perhaps did not, since Penny hadn't mentioned it.

Betty peered out again between the slats of the venetian blinds. The light was still on at Edward Kelso's house, but as she watched it snapped off and the house across the road was dark. She was alone on her little acre-size island of trees and grass and overgrown flowerbeds, sheltering in the old shingle house while unknown lives thrived in the strange seas that surrounded her.

Betty, however, was not entirely unknown to them.

The three Saks boys across the way quarreled over the Nintendo, the TV channel, the last slice of pepperoni pizza until Penny gave them The Look. They then wisely settled down to comparatively peaceful pursuits. Penny took control of the television set to watch "Entertainment Tonight" while their father picked up the latest *Sports Illustrated*.

"That Miss Trenka seems nice," Penny said with half an eye on a report of a popular young star's drug problems. "We should have her over to dinner next week."

Greg Saks was more interested in the Giants' chances for a winning season. "Think she'll agree to sit with the boys sometime? They're getting to be too much for that little high school girl."

Penny chuckled. "She looks like she could handle them." She raised her voice. "That's *enough*, Whitey."

On the other side of Timberhill Road Ted Kelso could see the lights on at the Saks house and the lights of his new neighbor. He hoped this woman who'd moved in wasn't an aggressive, neighborly type who felt she had to run over with some dreadful casserole for him from time to time.

Ted moved away from the windows out toward the back of his house, where he could readily ease through the kitchen door to the attached garage and into his car to drive to his dinner appointment. He much preferred to stay at home and do his own cooking, but Denise liked dining out and he liked to please her.

Some miles away Betty's soon-to-be employer Jerry Preston looked up from the papers he'd brought home from the office as his wife said, "I want—"

Since she already had most of the things that most people wanted, including a brand-new house with brand-new furnishings, a socially acceptable car, and even a new live-in nanny for their little girl, Jerry couldn't imagine what she wanted now. He said, "Not now, Nicole."

Nicole, petite, dark-haired, and well-formed by dint of assiduous exercise, ignored him. "I want to run over to the mall before the stores close," she said. "I want to look at some upholstery fabric for that woman I told you about.

The one who wants me to redo her house. Then I'll stop at the health club."

"I might go out myself," he said. "I want to go over to Zig-Zag to look at some of the new stuff the programmers are working on. I have an idea—"

"Are you planning to stay there until all hours again?" his wife asked with a trace of bitterness. Jerry knew she liked being the wife of the president of Zig-Zag, even if it was thanks to her father's money. She liked being queen of their modest country club. She did not like to be reminded that he was still a computer hacker at heart who'd never willingly lift a golf club with the guys or happily don a dinner jacket.

"Daddy says you can't concentrate on the business if you stretch yourself too thin," she said.

"Your father . . ." He stopped. "I'm responsible for Zig-Zag. I need to keep up with development so that I've got a solid negotiating position."

"You don't need to bargain," Nicole Preston said. "These people want what you've got. End of negotiations."

"Now *that* sounds like your father. He negotiates like a bulldozer. Denise is the diplomat. Did I tell you I found someone to fill in for her next week?"

"That woman thinks she's the boss, not you, and she takes too much time off. Don't forget we're going to Rhode Island early tomorrow. Please get in early enough to get some sleep. I don't want to visit our friends with a zombie." Nicole didn't wait to hear Jerry's answer to that.

In Denise Legrand's opinion, she took just the right amount of time off from her job. She worked long hours and often on weekends.

Denise sat at her dressing table in her bedroom in the big comfortable house she'd bought on Prospect Street in East Moulton and applied artful makeup. The little lines around her eyes were almost invisible. The sparing use of plastic surgery had helped defeat for a time the forces of age and gravity that had begun to prey on her chin. She definitely didn't look her age.

She smiled contentedly. Things were working out at last. Tomorrow she'd drive to New Haven and catch a Metro-North train to New York. Since it was Saturday, the cars wouldn't be full of business commuters. She had a reservation until Tuesday at the UN Plaza Hotel, just a couple of blocks from Grand Central Station. Business and pleasure. Perfect.

Denise combed her well-cut hair, carefully colored to mask the gray that was beginning to show up. She wore her new Donna Karan slacks and a tailored jacket over a bright Benetton shirt. Her low-heeled shoes were of soft leather, and the scent she dabbed on her wrists cost a hundred dollars an ounce, but it was worth it.

Downstairs, she went out the back door, leaving on the two lights on either side for her return. She walked around the house in the dark along the flagstone path, under the trees whose leaves were beginning to turn yellow and crimson. The thick clumps of golden and white chrysanthemums along the path were thriving in the cool, sunny autumn days.

She reached the end of the path and waited at the roadside. Prospect Street was dark. The houses along the winding road were set back and, like hers, surrounded by trees so that only glimpses of lighted windows could be seen. She imagined Alma Brown in her house at the top of the hill peering out to check on Ted's car as it stopped at Denise's house. Nosy old monster, but she didn't worry Denise.

It was so quiet she could almost hear the gurgle of the brook at the bottom of the hill where it cut across Prospect Street, spanned by a concrete bridge.

It was a very nice life she'd made for herself. Yes, Jerry Preston was something of an amiable fool, but he was easily managed. His father-in-law could be difficult, but she'd been able to get around him. There wasn't a problem she hadn't foreseen. Well, there was one problem. She disliked the idea of upsetting Ted Kelso, who'd been a good friend to her, but she'd figured out a way to handle that, too. She had her future to think about.

She waited for Ted's car to appear around the curve at the top of Prospect Street. It was a good idea to get him out of his house now and then.

Friday night slipped away for the citizens of East Moulton and the surrounding towns.

"I'm making progress, Cora," Betty told her former neighbor from Hartford on Saturday morning. Cora had called to see how Betty was getting on in the new place. "I've been at work all morning setting my house in order. Yes," she said, "it's nice to have a home of my own," and wasn't sure if it really was.

Cora said something about missing her and how nice the young couple who'd taken her apartment seemed to be. They were coming to brunch tomorrow.

"I'll be thinking of you," Betty said. She wondered how long Cora and Dave would continue to think of her.

A few cars passed her house as she continued to unpack. The straight stretch of road out front was a temptation to speeders. When a vehicle slowed down, she went to the window to look out. It was the mail carrier's van, which turned into Edward Kelso's driveway instead of stopping at his roadside mailbox. Moments later it backed out and proceeded on its way. There was no mail today for Betty.

She was amused that she had fallen into the trap that Dave Welles had warned her about: "The biggest thing that happens on a country road is somebody driving by." Even last night rather late, when the headlights of a car had shone through the blinds as it came up the hill, she'd gotten up to look. That car had turned into Mr. Kelso's driveway. It was nice to know that he did get about some, in spite of being "not well."

Saturday finally drew to a close, with the delivery of the afternoon edition of the *Ledger,* the local newspaper. A boy on a bicycle tossed it onto the lawn late in the day.

She settled down with it and a glass of sherry at the kitchen table.

WOMAN HIT-AND-RUN VICTIM. The small headline caught Betty's eye.

Longtime resident of East Moulton Denise Legrand, 52, of Prospect Street, was reportedly struck and killed by a speeding car as she walked near her home late Friday night. A witness claims to have seen a vehicle stop briefly and then drive on at or near the spot where Miss Legrand's body was discovered by a neighbor out jogging early Saturday morning.

Miss Legrand was a secretary at Zig-Zag Incorporated, Hammond Center.

Jerry Preston's secretary was now on permanent leave. How foresighted of him to have arranged for a temporary replacement in advance.

Betty looked up from her paper. How would Jerry Preston have seen her notice in the grocery store? She got out the brand-new telephone book the phone installer had left with her. A Gerald Preston was listed but in a new development ten miles away off the highway. Surely neither he nor his probable wife shopped at the modest East Moulton Supermarket and perused the bulletin board.

Denise Legrand, on the other hand, had been a longtime resident of the town. How ironic if Denise had put Jerry Preston on to Betty right before her death. Betty finished her sherry and put an excessively expensive frozen dinner in the microwave.

The day's unpacking activities had tired her more than she realized, and loneliness crept up again with the coming night. She resolutely turned on the television and watched a tearful Bette Davis find the stars and Paul Henreid on the classic black-and-white movie channel.

CHAPTER 3

SUNDAY WAS another sunny early-fall day. Betty toyed with the idea of taking a drive upstate to look at the foliage, which was beginning to turn into the colors of autumn. The red maple down the street in front of the Saks house looked redder than ever, and the oak trees beyond it had a definite touch of yellow in their leaves. As she looked out on the day, one Whitey Saks or another tore out of the family driveway on his bicycle and disappeared down the hill in the direction of the town center.

Betty wondered about the place where Denise Legrand had been killed. She remembered being shown a house on Prospect Street by the realtor. It was in the high-priced part of town, with houses too big for her on too much land along a winding rural road with lots of trees. Denise must have had grand tastes, and plenty of money to support them.

Then she told herself she wasn't really curious about seeing where Denise Legrand had died. She'd be better off locating a Sunday *Hartford Courant* and *New York Times* somewhere in East Moulton.

For years and years on Sunday mornings she'd habitually driven to the newspaper store to pick up the *Times* and the *Courant*. She liked to keep up-to-date on what was happening in the state and in the world beyond. Sometimes she would read them over coffee at the coffee shop next door to the newspaper store. Sometimes she'd bring them home to read after brunch with Cora and Dave Welles. She'd have to find new rituals.

Main Street was only a half-mile away. She ought to walk, in obedience to her doctor's admonitions about exercise, none of which she assumed he followed himself.

She decided to drive, in case she found that the drugstore didn't carry the *Times* and she had to go farther afield.

She might even take a look at Prospect Street.

Her silver-gray Buick was now parked at the side of the house. Last year, when it was time to replace her sensible eight-year-old Chevrolet, she'd looked at some flashy, low-slung Japanese cars in glowing red but had settled on the Buick. Then someone at Edwards & Son had called it "a mature car." She'd almost canceled the order and gone for a red one, but common sense had prevailed. At the moment the Buick stood in the driveway since the ramshackle single-car garage in back was crammed with several decades worth of detritus that the previous owners hadn't bothered to remove.

Another householder's chore to face, but later, after she'd read the papers. Maybe much later, like next spring.

Betty had found East Moulton a serviceable old Connecticut town, not especially quaint or charming. She'd chosen it almost at random. It was completely different from her old life, and far enough away from Hartford that she wouldn't be running back every chance she got. It had tree-lined streets and undistinguished clapboard and shingle homes set back from the road, with well-tended lawns and bright patches of flowers. Main Street was lined with small stores—the tailor and dry cleaner, a card shop, clothing store—all closed today except for the drugstore, which was open on Sundays until one, to sell papers and to fill overlooked prescriptions.

Cars were parked along the street in front of the white-steepled Congregational church across from the drugstore. The Catholic church was three streets away, and she understood that the Methodists had recently built a new church that was "too modern" for the taste of the realtor who had shown her around.

"You'd be Miz Trenka. Well, haven't I been looking forward to welcoming you to town."

Betty was startled to be greeted by name as she entered the drugstore. A middle-aged woman with a tired face and a floral smock beamed at her from behind the counter and then looked her up and down closely. Betty could almost read from her expression what she was thinking: Here's an odd old duck come to swim in our little pond. Funny clothes, and look at that hair.

At the office Betty had worn her hair pinned up, but at home she gathered it back and held it in place with an elastic band.

"I guess you're wondering how I know you," the woman said. "I'm Molly Perkins. Perk, that's the husband, is the pharmacist. We've run this place for donkey's years. An uncle of mine used to own the house you bought. He sold out to this young fellow who up and left his wife after a couple years." She sniffed as though to indicate a scandal not yet forgotten but scarcely proper to discuss right then. "The wife didn't want to stay on, so you'd have bought the place from her."

Betty nodded, not remembering from whom she had bought the house. The realtor and the seller's attorney had handled everything.

"So how are you finding it? I hope you don't have trouble with the furnace the way Unc did. A few years back it just went and died on him one winter. Coldest winter in memory. I think that's why he retired and moved to Florida. Didn't I hear that you're retired?"

Betty nodded unwillingly, but she was thinking more about the black monster of a furnace in her basement. The person who had inspected the house before she had bought it had said that everything was in good condition. Maybe she should have someone else in to look over the furnace before winter arrived.

Molly Perkins was on to a new subject. "I suppose you heard the awful news about Denise Legrand. Dead. Terrible, don't you think?"

"Yes, I read . . . I didn't know her, of course."

"Didn't you? She mentioned your name when she was in on Friday."

"Did she?" Betty was startled by this news.

"She said she'd heard you'd moved to town. She probably planned to welcome you. A saint. So good to her poor mother, may she rest in peace, and such a worker. The nicest woman you could meet. I cried when I heard. Of course, Denise wasn't a spring chicken, but you'd never have guessed it to look at her. Beautiful clothes she wore, always looked just so. Quite the glamour girl. Went to New York or Boston on weekends. That's where she got her clothes, although she always bought her makeup here and the little things a woman needs. She used to go off to Europe every few years."

It occurred to Betty that in the spirit of this cozy village chatter she might mention that she was going to work for a few days at Denise Legrand's company. Then she thought she wouldn't. She didn't want to become immediate gossip fodder for the town.

"I don't know how it could have happened," Molly went on. "That old road hasn't had a streetlight since the beginning of time, but Denise would have been careful walking in the dark. It's these kids and their cars. Drugs and drink. They're everywhere." Molly shook her head. "I've been talking away and haven't asked what you wanted."

"I'll take a *Courant*. And do you carry the *New York Times*?"

"We only get three copies for people in town. Wes Sampson, he's the lawyer, and Ted Kelso." She looked momentarily stricken. "And Denise. You could have hers today, poor thing. She won't be needing it."

"I'll take it every week," Betty said. Molly lifted the heavy newspaper from behind the counter. "Do you know anything about Zig-Zag, the company Miss Legrand worked for? It was mentioned in the paper."

"Top-secret stuff," Molly said. "Has to do with comput-

ers. The Hammonds never let grass grow under their feet,
I can tell you. Why, I remember years ago—"

"The woman's got it wrong again." The male equivalent
of Molly in age and weariness came up the aisle from the
back of the store. He was wearing a professional-looking
white jacket. He put out his hand. "Perk Perkins."

"This is Miz Trenka, bought Unc's old place. Just what
do I have wrong?"

"Computers yes. But nothing top secret. They do software for businesses. Small scale, but there's been talk about
expanding. That's what this area needs, what with the economy way down. Hope we'll be getting your business, Miz
Trenka."

"Elizabeth," Betty said. If she got the name in early, it
might stick, after all these years. "I do have one or two prescriptions." Who didn't nowadays, especially when the
years were making themselves felt with random aches and
pains, if not worse. "I'll have my doctor write up new ones
for you."

"Appreciate that," Perk said. A phone rang in the back of
the store. "Somebody just burned the roast and discovered
they were out of tranquilizers, I'll bet. See you again."

"There's a big chain drugstore over at the mall," Molly
said, "but we think we offer real personalized service. I'm
always dropping things off for Ted Kelso, right across from
your place." She said in a low voice meant to convey con-
fidentiality, "He has trouble getting about, you know. I go
over after business hours." She looked at Betty hopefully.

"Then you must stop in for a visit," Betty said with a
mildly sinking heart at the thought of endless gossip with
Molly. She wouldn't be entirely lonely, that was certain.
"When I've settled in a bit more."

"I'll do that. I've got my eye on you, Whitey."

Betty looked around and saw one of the Saks boys examining the candy bars. He looked up, angelically innocent.

"Does your mother know you're buying candy before
lunch?" Molly asked. "And will you take Mr. Kelso's paper
to him or am I going to be stuck doing it?"

Whitey stuck out his lower lip in a pout and went off to view the comic books in the magazine rack that ran along one wall. The copies of *Playboy* and *Penthouse* were well out of his reach.

"Denise used to take it around to him most Sundays, kind of a ritual it was, unless she was going to be out of town. Then I'd do it," Molly said. "She told me on Friday she'd be away this weekend. She and Ted were real good friends." She shook her head sadly.

"I could take it to him," Betty said quickly. She was glad of an excuse to meet her neighbor.

"Well, thank you. Just set it on the package shelf by the front door. You don't even have to ring the bell."

A sturdy, great-bosomed woman made a stately entrance into the drugstore. She looked like an actress whose name Betty couldn't remember who used to play sour matrons on old TV situation comedians.

"Here's Miz Brown," Molly said. "This is Elizabeth Trenka, Miz Brown. She's new in town. How was the sermon today?"

"Adequate." Mrs. Brown evidently disapproved. "I was shocked that the reverend even mentioned the Legrand woman's name. No better than she should be, and never was."

Betty was thinking that the late Denise Legrand did not seem to conform to the usual definition of a fifty-two-year-old unmarried secretary at a small company in a small town. The opinions on her ranged from saint to tramp, albeit a well-dressed one.

Mrs. Brown proceeded down an aisle devoted to over-the-counter remedies for everything from headaches to tired blood to bunions.

"She never liked Denise," Molly whispered. "That thing with her son, Alan," she added enigmatically. "It was years ago, and Denise left town and only came back when her mother got sick, but still . . ."

Since Mrs. Brown was returning to the register with an

item in her gloved hand, Molly fell silent. Betty decided to escape.

"If I could have Mr. Kelso's paper . . ."

"We'll see you again real soon," Molly said. Mrs. Brown nodded, dismissing the newcomer. Betty suspected that as soon as she departed, Molly would share her thoughts with Mrs. Brown: *A retired lady. Retired from what?* she'd like to know. *And she knew for a fact that her uncle's house wouldn't come cheap. Where did she get the money for it? She doesn't look wealthy, that's for sure, and not a bit of style. How old do you suppose she is?*

On and on the questions would go as curiosity spawned new ones, but at least, Betty thought with a grin, she couldn't have seemed to either woman to be no better than she should be.

CHAPTER 4

BETTY PUT the newspapers on the passenger seat and turned the ignition. There was more activity on Main Street now that the various churches in town had sent forth their congregations to the rewards of Sunday lunch and football games on television.

She could go home to the modest pleasures of the Sunday papers or she could succumb to the temptation of seeing Prospect Street. She'd always been curious about the whys and hows of ordinary and out-of-the-ordinary events. In running the office at Edwards & Son she had found it paid to understand how things came to happen and what was behind them. Business suffered when personal matters impinged too much on the work. She wasn't nosy—just curious.

Why would a reportedly fashionable, well-traveled middle-aged woman be walking on a country road late at night? And who indeed would also be about at that hour to witness a terrible hit-and-run accident? Who had found her?

She thought if she headed back toward her house and took a left at the crossroads near the grammar school, she would find herself close to Prospect Street.

The sign was almost obscured by the autumn-hued leaves of maples and oaks, but Betty recognized the street when she saw it. The house she'd been shown still had a For Sale sign on it. She drove the winding road slowly, as it dipped down and rose up on little hills. It was almost a single-lane road in places and the curves would be dangerous at night at high speed.

It seemed to her that anyone walking along this curving, hilly road could not have missed seeing the lights of a car coming from either direction.

At the bottom of a hill, where a bridge crossed a small stream, she saw the signs of police presence. Some strips of yellow plastic marked out the scene of the tragedy. The bridge railing had been knocked slightly askew, and the cement looked chipped.

She parked her car on the gravelly shoulder as far off the road as she could and got out, careful not to disturb the plastic strips.

There was nothing much to see. She listened to the sound of the brook gurgling over the stones in little waterfalls, then walked to the middle of the bridge and looked down at the flowing stream. Little eddies of foam swirled around under the bridge. It had been a fairly dry summer, but the springs that fed this brook seemed not to have been affected.

She paused to examine the bridge railing. It was bent slightly and the concrete was definitely chipped, but rust had begun to appear around the dents in the iron railing and the chipped concrete was weatherworn. Old damage then. Denise Legrand had certainly not been killed on the bridge proper by all appearances, but somewhere off to the side. There seemed to be no skid marks on the roadside, but, of course, she knew very little about accidents of this sort.

Back at the car, Betty paused to look back up Prospect Street. She wondered which of the large houses had belonged to Denise, but it was impossible to tell. The mailboxes had only numbers, no names.

She turned the ignition. She wanted to go back, feeling like a mere sensation-seeker exposing herself to the neighborhood's inspection from behind the curtains, but the road was too narrow to turn here. There seemed to be no place up ahead where she could pull in, turn the car, and retrace her route. With a sigh, she headed on into the unknown, across the narrow bridge.

The land was flatter here, and she caught a glimpse of an

old-fashioned red barn standing back in the fields. Then she came upon a produce stand set up at the side of the road in front of a white clapboard house with a big veranda.

All this would have been farmland in years gone by. It was only with the coming of suburbia that fashionable split-levels began to spring up among the fields and woodlands.

The pretty teenage girl who was minding the stand took off her earphones and shut off her Walkman to sell Betty three pounds of late tomatoes, a plump Hubbard squash, and a half-gallon of cider.

"I'm a little lost," Betty said. "If I keep on this road, will it take me back to town?"

The girl cocked her head. "You could turn back."

"I want to get to know my way about," Betty said. "I'm new to East Moulton."

The girl wrinkled her perfect little nose. "Why would anyone want to move here? All I can think about is getting out of here. Like, go to New York or Hollywood." There was a gleam in her eyes that did not bode well if her parents didn't like the idea of their daughter running off to the bright lights. She was about sixteen, tall and slim, with long, straight brown hair. She was wearing tight jeans and a short denim jacket liberally studded on the sleeves and front with rows of silver and rhinestone studs. Very likely she saw herself as a trendy model or a hot starlet ripe for the silver screen.

"I'm Elizabeth Trenka," Betty said. "I bought the house that used to belong to Molly Perkins's uncle."

"Her. She likes to know everybody's business."

"And what's your name?" Betty asked, since the girl didn't seem inclined to mention it.

"Evangeline," she said grandly. "You like it?"

"Well, if it's your name . . ."

"It's not. It's Evelyn, but that's *too* dull. Sometimes I call myself Eve. *Not* Evie. That's what my mother calls me. I hate it."

"I understand about names, Eve," Betty said. "Oh, I do.

I suppose you knew Miss Legrand, the lady who was killed the other night."

Eve looked away. "Yeah, sure. From up the hill. The big white house with the green trim. She used to buy things from us." Her profile suggested some inner turmoil brought on by the mention of Denise's death. Young people could be deeply affected by encountering death in real life, as opposed to the empty images on television.

"A terrible thing," Betty said kindly, "when a friend dies."

"She wasn't my friend exactly," Eve said, "but she was real nice to me." She seemed to be breathing rapidly, as though in the throes of continued agitation. "She gave me some dresses. Mom made me give them back, but they were beautiful. She was a . . ." She sought the right words. "She was a woman of the world. I want to be like her."

Betty heard the yearning in her voice to be like Denise Legrand, with all her imagined worldly freedom and luxurious worldly goods.

"You can be anything you want, but it takes time," Betty said. She knew that sometimes it didn't work out the way one planned, but sometimes it did: that little girl at Edwards & Son a few years back who was determined to go to business school and was now a senior vice president of a big firm in the Midwest; her old high school friend who had the looks and the will to become briefly a famous model with her face in every fashion magazine. Then there was Betty, who had wanted to go to college, but when she was young, girls with fathers like hers didn't think about going to college. If they were lucky, they went to secretarial school and prayed they'd find a husband. She'd had her chance at that, but not at a formal education.

"I sure don't want to be selling vegetables all my life," Eve was saying. Her agitation had given way to a kind of petulant anger. "Nobody around here lives on a farm anymore. The kids at school think it's a joke. My father could sell his land and let them build houses and we'd be rich. People do it all the time, like those nice houses over in

Hodders Woods. But no. He goes, 'Marry a good honest fellow who loves the land and leave those wild boys alone,' and I go, 'Me, marry a farmer?' " She shuddered.

Betty suspected that Eve's boyfriends were a source of contention between Eve and her father.

"I want to end up living with a real cute guy and have lots of money, someplace where it never snows and where there are clubs and dancing all night." This sounded defiant, like the last shouted words of an argument designed to drive her father to rage. Then a strangely cunning look appeared on her pretty young face. "I'll do it, too. I figured out a way . . ." She stopped.

Betty decided it was time to move away from Eve's vision of the future. She didn't know much about teenage girls who acted on their craving for the bright lights, but it had to mean trouble somewhere.

"I wonder, who found Miss Legrand's body?" Betty asked cautiously. She didn't want to upset Eve again.

Eve answered quickly. "Alan Brown. He runs in the morning with his dog. He lives at the top of the hill. With his *mother*." She sounded disgusted. "I used to see . . ." She stopped. "I see him all the time because I get up so early."

Betty registered the name Brown. Surely it must be the same Mrs. Brown who had had nothing good to say about Denise. And Alan was the son who had given her cause to dislike Denise.

"They said in the paper that somebody actually saw the accident happen," Betty said.

"No! Nobody saw anything. The police didn't ask me anything. Nobody's around here in the middle of the night. Some kid made up a story, that's all." Eve fiddled nervously with her earphones and took a deep breath. Betty saw fear in her eyes. "If you want to get back to the center of town, keep on this road and make a left the first chance you get. Half a mile." She put on the earphones and turned on her Walkman, resolutely shutting out Betty and her questions.

Betty drove on. It had been another view of Denise

Legrand to add to her collection of images: a young girl's idea of a woman of the world, but there was something more unsettling. Eve's fear. She could imagine Eve creeping out of the big farmhouse late at night to meet a boyfriend along the dark road or in the woods beside the brook. She could imagine the couple hidden among the trees seeing Denise, seeing the car and the accident—or seeing something. The state of the bridge bothered her and the fact that Denise should have seen the oncoming car. Eve might not have risked a statement to the police that would get her into trouble with her parents, but an anonymous call to the police? Or the boy might have told someone . . .

Stop it, she told herself. You're fantasizing. It's none of your business.

The *Times* was dutifully left on the wide shelf just outside Edward Kelso's door. According to Molly Perkins, Denise had planned to be away for the weekend, but the accident had put an end to that. Her good friend Edward Kelso—Molly had called him Ted—had probably known about her plans. And he'd surely heard by now that she was dead. Betty wondered if her sickly neighbor was in need of anything, although she would be the first to admit that she wasn't good at providing comfort during a time of grief.

I won't intrude, she decided. Then she paused. Edward Kelso had been out late on Friday night in his car.

Late in the afternoon she looked out a front window and saw that the newspaper was gone from Ted Kelso's front door.

CHAPTER 5

THE BUILDING occupied by Zig-Zag Incorporated in the Hammond Center Office Park sat on a grassy knoll, carefully landscaped with clusters of young pines and mountain laurel bushes. It was a low, modern concrete box with tinted windows and looked very much like a suburban high school, lacking only the requisite playing fields. She had passed a few similar buildings on the newly constructed road from the minimall that seemed to constitute most of Hammond Center. The Hammonds that Molly Perkins had mentioned must be the local landowners who had given their name to the hamlet.

A parking lot at the side held only one car at eight-thirty on Monday morning. Betty parked her car at the far side of the lot. Executives were touchy about people taking the choice spots near the front door they thought they were entitled to.

The heavy glass door swung open, as promised.

Betty experienced a sense of familiarity as she entered the building. It was all much more modern than the offices of Edwards & Son, of course, but the faint hum of air circulating was well remembered, as was the stark white light from the overhead fluorescent bulbs and the expectant silence before the arrival of chattering clerks and secretaries and the rumble of decision-making executive voices. Betty had often arrived at work well before everyone else and accomplished much in that quiet time before the phones began to ring and the unexpected problems of administration flooded in.

The curved receptionist's desk was unoccupied. The sleek telephone console had one light on, indicating that Jerry Preston must be making an early-morning call. The receptionist's computer screen was dark.

Modern chocolate-brown and chrome chairs arranged around a low glass-topped table formed an impersonal grouping for office visitors. The large potted rubber plants had glossy leaves, which suggested that the receptionist devoted time to tending them. Abstract lithographs that matched the decor hung on the beige paneled walls. It looked new and prosperous, if somewhat unimaginative.

"Hello?" she called out tentatively. She peered down the two bright corridors, but all of the doors were closed. In the face of the silence, her self-assurance was diminishing. She was at her best when she was in charge. Now she was a stranger faced with the unknown. Betty conquered a brief wave of uncertainty. She kept her eye on the light on the phone console and waited beside the receptionist's desk.

What would be the general state of mind in the office, she wondered, following the sudden death of a colleague? Did the staff view Denise Legrand as Molly Perkins's "saint," Mrs. Brown's shady lady, Eve's woman of the world, or perhaps someone entirely different? Kindly or demanding, remote or one of the gang?

Based on her long experience in handling office crises like a sudden death, she knew that her first day at Zig-Zag would not be business as usual. At least it was not her problem. She had no knowledge of the attitude of the people who would cluster at the water cooler or around a desk whispering their memories of the dead woman.

Behind the scenes there were sure to be readjustments, as people jockeyed to fill the void to their best advantage. Tragedy heightened the usual stresses among people who were connected only by their jobs. Of course, there were always occasions when the personal relationships that flowed hidden beneath the surface were shattered by the unexpected. That time when Sid Senior had had his heart attack and she'd been sure he would die . . .

"You must be Betty." Jerry Preston was in his thirties, quite a handsome fellow, she thought, in a shaggy way, but he looked as though he hadn't slept well. He was definitely not her idea of a company president in his blue jogging suit and high-tech running shoes, but these days she knew things were different from Edwards & Son's conservative practices.

Betty herself had dressed carefully, in her favorite light-wool heather-gray suit with the very nice pearl button earrings Sid Senior had bought her years ago. Flat shoes, of course. The years had taught her that a woman who towered excessively over her superiors put herself at risk of appearing dangerously intimidating or, worse, insubordinate.

"Mr. Preston? Good morning."

His handshake was tentative. He immediately released her hand and brushed his hair back off his forehead in a nervous gesture. His look of inspection gave his thoughts away: She's not young. Odd-looking but not threatening. Well dressed. Seems together; not a crazy.

"Um, well. Welcome aboard. Let me just show you around, and you can tell me about your background. We need all the help we can get." Jerry headed toward one of the corridors. "It's not going to be such a great day, I'm afraid," he said. "My right-hand woman, Denise Legrand, was killed in an accident over the weekend. It hit me hard. She's ... she was something else."

Betty tried to hear sincere grief in his voice, but it wasn't there. Nervousness, however, was. Surely it wasn't she who was unnerving him.

Behind them all of the phone lines suddenly seemed to start ringing at once. Jerry stopped and looked back, just as a Federal Express delivery man came through the door with an armload of overnight envelopes. Jerry made a tentative move toward the phones.

"George," he said, sounding surprised. Betty saw that another man, this one in a business suit, had come barreling through the door like an angry bear. He was big, like a football player years out of training and running to fat. He had a reddish face and thinning hair. He was much closer to Betty's age than to Jerry's.

The phones kept ringing.

"Preston, we've got to talk. Now." The man grabbed Jerry's arm and started to hustle him away. "Mitsui flew into New York on Friday. He's sure to show up here. Are you ready?"

"I didn't know that, George. I ..." Jerry looked confused. "I thought you were out in California. No one said you were back."

"Well, I am back. I asked if you were ready for Mitsui. He must have found out something. I tried to get you during the weekend."

"We were away. The phones—"

"Damn the phones." George was scowling.

"Let me handle things, Mr. Preston," Betty said. "Shall I say you're not in yet?"

"Please," Jerry said. "Marsha and Tanya and Eileen will be here any minute. George, Denise isn't here."

Betty picked up the phone and signaled the Federal Express man to bring her the envelopes. "Zig-Zag, please hold." Fortunately, the hold button was clearly marked.

She heard George say as he hustled Jerry away, "Denise is at the bottom of this. She's the one who told me about Mitsui."

"But she's dead," Jerry said, and then they were gone.

"Zig-Zag, please hold," Betty said to the next caller, and picked up the third call. "Zig-Zag, good morning. No, Mr. Preston isn't in yet. I'll give him the message." She jotted down a name and a number and picked up one of the calls on hold. "May I help you?" She spoke on the phone as she scanned the pile of overnight envelopes and signed for them. "Mr. Preston isn't in yet. Cancel lunch today?" She made another note. "I'll tell his secretary. Yes." Well, she'd tell somebody, since Jerry Preston no longer had a secretary or whatever title Denise had worn.

The Federal Express man finished punching in codes on

his handheld device and gave her a wave as he sauntered out.

She picked up the last call on hold. "Sorry to keep you waiting . . ." She listened. "Yes, Marsha," she said when there was a pause in the flow of words and questions. "Mr. Preston mentioned you. Yes, I'm the temp. I did hear about Miss Legrand. Now, dear, you mustn't take it so hard." Yet another call came in. "Let me put you on hold, Marsha, while I answer another call." The poor girl sounded quite distraught. "Zig-Zag, good morning." She listened. "Let me check if he's come in."

She spoke to Marsha again. "Can you tell me how to reach Mr. Preston by intercom from the front desk? I see. Wait one more minute." Betty found the list of intercom extensions beside the console.

She was about to press the button that would put her through to Jerry Preston when the door flew open and a young woman with deliberately disordered hair and quite a bit of makeup marched in.

"Who are you?" she demanded.

Instead of answering, Betty spoke to Jerry Preston. "A man with the resident state trooper's office is on the line. He needs to speak with you urgently. Very good."

"I asked what you thought you were doing," the young woman said in a manner meant to convey hostile authority, although it sounded merely petulant.

"No," Betty said. "You asked who I was. What I am doing seems obvious." She picked up Marsha's call. "I'm sorry. Things are a bit hectic here. I'm sure Mr. Preston will understand." She listened to the distraught Marsha. "A word to the wise," she said finally. "I'd be careful about making rash statements. We'll see you tomorrow."

The young woman had taken off her coat and flung it over her shoulder. She was tapping her foot impatiently. Betty noted that she was what used to be called shapely. She wasn't sure what the term was now for a buxom lass with a very short skirt cinched at the waist, a clinging blouse in a particularly violent purple, and an excess of chunky jewelry.

Betty took off her glasses and said, "I am Elizabeth Trenka. I am here to work temporarily for a few days. Is there something I can do for you?" Stern but kind. It was usually effective with excitable young women. At first.

"No. I mean, I work here. Amanda Glyn, Jerry's personal assistant," she said, and defied Betty to deny it.

Another one? Betty thought, or a case of The Queen Is Dead, Long Live Amanda?

"I was just surprised to see you," Amanda said. "You don't look like . . . I mean, Jerry didn't mention that he was getting a temp while Denise was away."

"That's the way men are," Betty said. "They will go off and make independent decisions."

Amanda looked at her sharply. Betty did not betray a smile.

"Um, well. Yes," Amanda said. She was grudgingly apologetic.

"Now," Betty said briskly as she stood, towering over the petite Amanda, "I'm not sure what Mr. Preston intends for me. I do know that Marsha won't be coming in today."

"Oh? What's her excuse this time?"

Betty looked at her. "Denise Legrand."

"Denise? Marsha didn't have anything to do with Denise, except they were kind of chummy sometimes."

"Denise is dead," Betty said. "Didn't you know?"

The smug smile on Amanda's face told Betty that she was well aware of the situation.

"No kidding?" she said. She arched her eyebrows as though receiving a startling bit news. "Do they know who did it?"

Betty wasn't at all impressed by her feigned surprise. "It was an accident. Hit-and-run on Friday night, near her home. Surely you heard. Everyone else has."

"You hear a lot of things," Amanda said slyly. "At least I do. I'd better see Jerry. He'll be needing me." She started away, dragging her coat behind her.

Betty didn't miss her brief look of triumph. "He's with someone named George," she said.

"George is here? He's supposed to be in Los Angeles."

"Nevertheless—" The phone diverted her. "Zig-Zag. Good morning." Betty was at ease with the phone system now. "Mr. Preston isn't in yet. Ah, Mrs. Preston." Amanda pointed frantically at herself. "One moment."

Amanda grabbed the receiver from Betty.

"Nicole? It's Amanda. He's in a meeting with Mr. Hammond. Absolutely no calls." She listened. "Hold on. I'd better take this in my office." She leaned over again, pushed the hold button, and replaced the receiver in its cradle. "Bitch," she said, and flounced off down the corridor. Betty presumed the reference was to Jerry Preston's wife and not to herself. Seconds later the flashing light stopped as Amanda picked up the call elsewhere.

George Hammond? Of the Hammond Center Office Park? Apparently a man of some importance, considerably agitated about the imminent arrival of a Mr. Mitsui, whom Jerry had to be ready for, but his "right-hand woman" Denise had died at an untimely moment on a dark road. The day was certainly well begun.

A pert, dark-haired girl flew in breathlessly, loaded down with a satchel and a handbag. "Hi, I'm Eileen, you must be the temp. Denise said somebody would be coming." She tossed her head in the direction of a middle-aged man who came into the building behind her. "This is Mr. Caruso in sales. I'm not too late today, am I, Mr. Caruso?"

He nodded and almost winked at Betty as he went about his business.

"He's okay, kind of an old stick. I didn't hear your name."

"Betty . . . Elizabeth Trenka."

"You look kinda old to be temping," Eileen said as she dumped her satchel on the floor beside the desk. "What kind of name is that? Trenka."

"It goes back to Czechoslovakia," Betty said. "My grandfather—"

"Did you hear about Denise?" Eileen was arranging a pile of magazines on the floor beside the receptionist's chair: *Glamour*, *Redbook*, *Allure*, *People*, *The National Enquirer*. "What a shock. Marsha called me up Saturday, just when Billy came to pick me up. We were going to the mall. I was nearly sick to my stomach. She had these great clothes, you know? I wonder who gets them now."

"It must have been a shock—"

"Yeah. She kind of ran everything here. Well, somebody will show you around. Marsha, probably."

"Marsha isn't coming in today," Betty said. "She's upset about Miss Legrand."

Eileen stopped fussing with her magazines and looked at Betty, chewing the inside of her cheek as she processed the news.

"Naw," she said finally. "She didn't like Denise all that much. One of her kids probably got sick. Or maybe Mikie pasted her one and she doesn't want to show a black eye again in the office."

Betty was mildly shocked at Eileen's casual acceptance of domestic violence. There had been a couple of cases of it over the years at Edwards & Son, and Betty had sat the victims down and talked them into getting counseling in one case and escaping in another.

Eileen flipped through a desk calendar. "Mr. P. has lunch today. I better remind Denise." She caught herself and looked distressed. "I forgot."

"Lunch was canceled. I left a note there on the desk. But Miss Glyn came in earlier. I suppose she should be told, if she's now his personal assistant."

Eileen made a face full of contempt. "Doesn't she wish? She's just a typist, but she'll be glad to handle everything *personally*. She tries to give orders, but I don't let her get away with anything. I know my job description by heart."

"Mr. Hammond seems to have arrived unexpectedly," Betty said.

"Uh-oh," Eileen said. "I'd better stow the magazines until Mr. Big Guy is out of the way."

"Is Hammond Center named for his family?"

Eileen shrugged. "They say. Here's Tanya. She'll take care of you." Three lines started ringing. "These phones never quit."

As Eileen took care of the incoming calls, Betty said quickly, "Mr. Preston isn't taking calls yet," then turned to face the well-put-together young black woman Eileen had called Tanya. It was difficult to tell whether she was twenty, thirty, or forty, but she was considerably younger than Betty.

"Elizabeth Trenka," Betty said. She thought to put out her hand and then decided not to. Tanya was looking her up and down and did not seem entirely pleased with what she saw.

Eileen finished with the calls and said, "Can we call you Betty? Elizabeth sounds so . . . so old."

Betty nodded. She would never be Elizabeth here at Zig-Zag.

"Let's go,' Tanya said. "I could use your help."

"Hey, Tanya," Eileen said. "You didn't say what you think about Denise. You heard, right?"

Tanya shrugged. "You live and then you die. No big thing. Somebody finally had enough of her and drove a car into her."

"What an *awful* thing to say!" Eileen was wide-eyed. Betty thought she couldn't be more than eighteen or nineteen. "She never did a thing to you."

"Not lately," Tanya said.

Betty said nothing, but Marsha had said something similar on the phone about Denise Legrand: Someone had intentionally ended her life.

CHAPTER 6

BETTY FOLLOWED Tanya down the other corridor to an ergonomically correct room with several computers humming quietly, their screens darkened. Near the end of her days at Edwards & Son, Sid Junior had commanded Betty to order this sort of modern computer furniture. Yes, she had argued the expense and then had surrendered to the demands of the new boss.

"Yo. Betty girl. Are you working here or dreaming the day away?" Tanya had brought up a screen on her computer.

"Sorry," Betty said.

"I hope you can handle a computer," Tanya said. "We're way behind on our billing." She looked at Betty doubtfully, as though it could not be possible that anyone over thirty could use a computer.

"I've had quite a bit of office experience," Betty said. "Very recently. But I think . . ." She stopped. What she thought was that Jerry Preston would likely demand her services, but her job now was not to state opinions of that sort. She wasn't in charge any longer.

"We're on-line with the warehouse in New Haven for incoming orders," Tanya said. "All you got to do is process them. Jerry did the programming. It's real easy to figure out, sort of a spreadsheet thing just for us. Know about Lotus? Good, you won't have any trouble then. He's a software genius, everybody says. Company name, account number. Mostly dealers, a few individuals. Discounts and shipping costs are all programmed in. There are always

special requests and problems, but don't worry about them.
I'll take care of them. Right now I got payables to worry
about." She shrugged. "Sit at Marsha's workstation."

Betty sat where Tanya instructed her to. There was a
framed picture of a girl and a boy on either side of a handsome but unsmiling thirtyish man. A little tray with a picture of Snoopy on it held a single earring, paperclips. A
child's crayon drawing was taped above the monitor.

Betty pondered briefly how to frame her question. "What
exactly does Zig-Zag do?"

"Just software," Tanya said. "Programs for businesses."
She seemed to be viewing Betty with some suspicion.
Temps didn't need to know anything.

"I suppose you'll all be going to the funeral," Betty said.

Tanya was hard-eyed. "I suppose. Let's get to work."

Betty got to work. A little trial, a little error, a few curt
instructions from Tanya left her feeling potentially compe-
tent but definitely still finding her way. It had been a long
time since she had been at the bottom of the personnel
heap.

After an hour Betty looked up from the screen where the
amber cursor throbbed peacefully at an entry for twenty
thousand dollars worth of software whose purpose was not
yet clear to her. The press of a key would produce discounts, shipping costs, and terms, and the printer would
produce an invoice with the customer's name, address, and
account number. Somewhere in a distant city another
printer would produce a bill of lading, a shipping label.

Tanya spoke briefly to someone on the intercom, then
said, "I got to run out on an errand. Any problems with that
stuff? No? Just leave anything you can't figure out until I
get back."

She did not, Betty noted, take her coat or handbag when
she left, so she wasn't planning to leave the building.

After a while the accounts room at Zig-Zag Incorporated
began to seem unnervingly quiet. Betty went to the door
and listened. The corridor was quiet, too. There were no
voices, no phones, no people to be seen.

A quarter of an hour later Tanya had not returned. Betty decided to venture forth to find coffee, the ladies' room, another human being.

The reception area was empty. Eileen's magazines were still piled on the floor beside her chair. Betty went back down the corridor and tried the doors. One, two, three empty offices, and none of them apparently heavily used. At the end of the hall she found the ladies' room and near it a room with a huge copier, the fax machine, a table with a pot of coffee in the coffeemaker, and a small refrigerator (nearly empty, except for cans of a liquid-diet substance).

Betty retraced her steps to the reception area and walked cautiously down the second corridor, the one Jerry Preston and George Hammond had taken. She knocked on the doors and listened before opening them, but she needn't have been concerned. None of them was occupied.

In an office with two desks she saw Amanda's coat and bag. In another a blue jogging shirt tossed over the back of a chair indicated that it was Jerry Preston's office. A smaller office, with a door to the corridor and a second one opening into Jerry's was evidently that of the late Denise Legrand. It was nicely furnished—not coldly modern like Jerry's and the others she'd seen. It had a warm feeling, as though its occupant had taken pains to make it a personal place. A pair of lovely watercolors of famous Roman scenes were on one wall, and the faint scent of expensive perfume hung in the air as a ghostly reminder of Denise.

Her office window looked out on clusters of carefully planted trees and a couple of benches in their shade. Denise must have been good with plants: a row of luxuriant, healthy houseplants in big multicolored ceramic pots stood on a low table before the window. It was the kind of office Betty would have enjoyed but never had. Her desk at Edwards & Son, year in, year out, had been in a cramped room between Sid Senior's office and the big room of cubicles with head-high partitions where the office staff worked.

Betty found a few more empty offices and tried a locked door marked PROGRAMMING RESTRICTED.

The only door left to try was one at the end of the corridor. As she headed toward it, the door burst open and George Hammond stamped out. He slammed the door behind him and brushed past her without a word. She could see a vein throbbing in his temple and his face was redder than ever. Not healthy, she thought. The place was going to end up being the Hammond Center Memorial Park if George Hammond wasn't careful.

She tried the handle of the door he'd emerged from.

They were all there seated around the table in the middle of a big conference room: Tanya, Eileen, Amanda. Mr. Caruso. A tall boy in jeans and a T-shirt. A couple of men similarly dressed. Jerry Preston stood at the head of the long table.

They looked like deer caught in the headlights, with frightened eyes fixed on her as she stood in the doorway.

Betty opened her mouth to apologize for intruding, but all she could think of was whether Denise Legrand had looked the way they did when the car sped toward her. Terrified. But no, she couldn't have. She wouldn't have walked into the headlights of an oncoming car. Betty already knew that Denise would have seen the headlights coming over the hill long before . . .

"Ah . . . Betty. Yes." Jerry Preston rubbed his hands nervously. "We were just discussing . . . That is, the office intends to do something. For Denise . . ."

"Can I go now, Jerry?" Amanda tossed her hair, but it did not improve it. "Mr. Hammond wants me to do some stuff before he takes off again." She stood up and brushed close to him as she headed for the door.

Jerry drew back to avoid touching her. "Yes. Take good care of Mr. Hammond, by all means. We all ought to get back to work. Betty, could I see you in my office?"

She nodded. The body language of the employees of Zig-Zag definitely expressed high tension as they filed out.

"Right in here," Jerry said, and ushered her into the office she had already identified as his. "I wonder if you would help me with some letters? Denise used to see that my correspondence was taken care of, but if you don't mind taking down some words?"

It was Betty's inclination to remark that she didn't really have any say in the matter, one way or the other. The inclination was stifled, and she thought she could manage a bit of dictation, although her shorthand was rusty.

"I suppose you're wondering about our little meeting," Jerry said. He slumped in the leather chair behind his desk.

"No," Betty said firmly. "I was wondering about nothing, and if I were, it's none of my business." She watched Jerry Preston through the thick lenses of her tortoise-rim glasses.

She was actually wondering about the remarkably small group that seemed to occupy the fairly spacious Zig-Zag building. Perhaps George Hammond had other tenants. She also wondered exactly what a "personal assistant" along the lines of an Amanda Glyn would do about the place. Those very long red nails of hers must make it difficult to pick out the letters on a keyboard. Mostly she was wondering about Denise Legrand, about this Mr. Mitsui looming on the horizon, and about why a significant percentage of the office staff thought Denise had had it coming to her. She couldn't think of a way to probe without seeming too nosy for a temporary typist.

"You're right," he said at last. "Our little problems shouldn't concern you." He looked miserable, and so young. It would take years for him to figure out that a lot of things didn't matter as much as he thought. "We'll finish up these letters and then I'll be leaving for the day. I have to see . . . see some people."

"Before we get started," Betty said, "I wonder if you could tell me how you happened to find me. See my notice, that is."

"It was Denise. She saw it at some grocery store last Thursday. Said you sounded perfect. Well . . ." He shrugged. "She didn't trust Amanda to handle things.

Mandy's a nice enough kid, but she needs a little more experience."

Betty was inclined to think that Amanda had plenty of a certain kind of experience.

Then Betty got down to work. She sent three short faxes for Jerry, and located several files without difficulty. The one lengthy letter she'd typed up had been, in his words, "perfect." Naturally. She'd rearranged some words to give it a more polished sound. He hadn't noticed her small changes, or at least hadn't mentioned them.

"I relied on Denise," Jerry Preston said in the middle of dictating another entirely routine letter Betty could have drafted herself with only a bit of instruction on Zig-Zag's corporate approach to correspondence. "Not that you're not doing just fine," he added quickly.

"I appreciate that," Betty said.

"She understood the business," Jerry said. He got up from his big chair and stared gloomily out the window. He turned around suddenly and spread out his arms to encompass his office: the slippery black leather sofa and the two bright red and chrome chairs, the big abstract paintings and a tortured twist of metal on a pedestal that probably represented a computer's internal organs as a clever way of referring to the company's business. Jerry had two slick black computer monitors on his desk.

"My wife handled the decorating," he said. "She tells me that neo-neo-modern offices have a power look." He shrugged. "Denise wouldn't let anyone touch hers."

"A mind of her own," Betty murmured.

"I'll say. And a good person really. She never married so she could take care of her mother who was sick for years and finally died a few years ago. Who could just run a person down like that? It was a terrible accident . . ." He stopped and looked at her as though he wanted her to agree wholeheartedly.

"Mr. Preston," Betty said softly. "I have a definite impression that people here think that it wasn't an accident. They think Denise was intentionally run down." She herself had strong doubts that the hit-and-run story was true, but it wasn't her place to mention it, and if the authorities chose to view it as that kind of accident, so be it.

"Who's saying that?" he asked sharply.

"No one's stating it as a fact. Marsha said something on the phone. Tanya and Amanda seem to take it as a given."

"She wasn't all that popular with the girls," Jerry said miserably, "because she was older, but she was one smart woman. I don't know what I'll do without her. It must have been an accident." He was still begging for her to agree.

"It probably was," Betty said in her best soothing voice. "You hear about these drunk drivers. . . ."

"I have to go over to East Moulton to talk to the police," Jerry said. "They have some questions. They tried to find me over the weekend, but Nicole and I were away." He looked hopeless. "I can't afford to get mixed up in"—he hesitated—"in a murder. I've got some delicate negotiations coming up this week."

"Mr. Mitsui?" Betty asked, and then wished she hadn't.

Pleasant, young Jerry Preston withdrew behind a wall, and his expression hardened with suspicion. "How do you know about him?" His eyes flickered toward the door, as though he were seeing the nosy new temp rifling through confidential files while supposedly on an innocent errand for him.

She wondered if her already limited employment at Zig-Zag was going to be shorter still. Then she had a truly liberating thought: It didn't matter.

So she said, "Young man, I've been in business a long time. I've had to learn the habit of hearing things and reviewing them and drawing conclusions. I think a capable professional does that. I've certainly not been prying into your business and shall not mention Mr. Mitsui again. I have no idea who he is."

He relaxed. A little.

"We may be doing a deal with him," he said. "Denise seemed to understand what he was really saying. They had a real rapport. I don't get these Japanese businessmen." He looked at her speculatively, as though measuring her ability to understand the Japanese the way Denise had.

"I'm afraid I've had no experience with the Japanese," Betty said. "The best I can say is I've seen some of the classic Japanese movies. I've read some books, and I read the newspaper."

"Books and papers don't tell you anything." He looked at his watch. "I've got to get over to East Moulton. I don't know if I'll be back. You can work with Tanya this afternoon, if you don't mind. It's probably not what you're accustomed to."

"I don't mind a bit." Betty stood up and closed the old-fashioned steno notebook she'd discovered in the supply room, while he put on a trench coat with lots of tabs and buckles.

She hesitated before leaving Jerry's office. "I understand you're a computer programmer," she said. Tanya had said he had a reputation as a software genius.

"A bit more than that. I design new software. Real advanced stuff. I used to, anyhow. I'd stay up all night, all day, all night again until I got it right. It was like trying to discover a cure for AIDS or cancer. You know that with just a little more time, you'll have it." He stopped and his face lighted up. "Then one day I had it, a cure for what ails software. It's perfect. Nobody's done it quite this way before. It's still supposed to be top secret, but it's going to be a sensation when we release it. I hope Zig-Zag can handle it."

"You've been in business awhile then?" Betty said.

"My father-in-law helped me start Zig-Zag a couple years ago to market some other software I'd developed. We're doing all right with that, but we have to get ready for the big release. My guys are doing the final debugging. I worry that people have gotten wind of it. Suddenly we have Mitsui coming around negotiating to acquire the software already on the market. I don't know what he really wants." He shrugged. "And I've got to deal with him alone, without Denise. I don't want to bring my father-in-law in. He doesn't really understand the implications of the new product, and besides, he made me responsible for the company. Denise was a big help. I'm going to miss her."

"Was she with you long?"

"Since we started. A friend of my wife's recommended her. She'd been away working in New York, but came back when her mother needed her. When she died, Denise wanted to stay in the area, so she jumped at the chance of working here. Just what she was looking for." He had a rueful look. "I have to admit that Denise liked being in charge. I was thinking of making her vice president. Even with Denise, though, I didn't have time for the real creative work anymore. I still fool around here with the programmers some nights, check on what they're doing." Now he had a faraway look, as though he was thinking of the days when he could put his mind into the intricacies of creating programs no one else had thought of. "My wife likes me being a full-time executive. Better for the image at the country club. I shouldn't be bothering you with all this," he said. "You're a good listener."

Betty didn't tell him that she'd been listening to executives talk out their troubles and triumphs for longer than he'd been alive.

The door to his office opened. Amanda wore what Betty thought of as a coyly ingratiating smile that was definitely not directed at her. "Mr. Hammond is finished with me. He said to tell you he's going home," she said. "Anything I can do for you?"

"Nothing. Betty has been very helpful. Don't forget the funeral is tomorrow at ten in East Moulton."

Jerry was collecting his briefcase, so he didn't see the look of distaste on Amanda's face.

"It's important to follow the traditional forms for our arrivals and departures," Betty said to fill the moment.

Amanda looked at her as though she were marginally batty.

Jerry looked up. "Arrivals and departures. Well said."

"Jerry . . ." Amanda almost simpered. She put out her

hand to touch his arm but drew it back quickly when she met Betty's eyes.

"I don't want to go either, Amanda, but we must. Say, Betty, could you handle this place alone tomorrow for a couple of hours?" His grin was genuine. "No, that's a dumb question. Of course you can."

CHAPTER 7

BETTY STARTED to follow Jerry Preston from his office. Amanda said, "Just a second. Sit down."

Betty looked at her, amazed at her boldness, and declined to sit. Amanda walked around to Jerry's chair and sat behind his desk. She waited, but Betty still did not sit, being unaccustomed to obeying the commands of unaccredited commanders. Amanda was clearly a young woman who had set her cap for the boss and Denise's job and didn't want any competition. Betty didn't want to become involved in some kind of *All About Eve* situation. She just wanted to find Tanya and get back to work.

"Exactly what were you and Jerry up to?" Amanda asked.

"Business as usual," Betty said, but she was thinking that this was really too much. "I must get back to work."

"Denise was no big loss," Amanda said, "but don't start thinking you're going to replace her."

Betty almost chuckled. "It never occurred to me, and please don't turn this into a third-rate melodrama. I understand that you have certain ambitions, but I am not here to hinder them. I shall be gone after Wednesday, according to my agreement with Mr. Preston. If you act with restraint, you might stand a chance of filling Miss Legrand's shoes."

"I wouldn't mind," Amanda said. "I couldn't stand her, but she sure knew how to operate. She had everybody fooled. Jerry, anyhow."

Betty attempted once more to depart.

To her eyes, Amanda Glyn looked like nothing more

than an overly made-up little girl playing at big-time office politics.

"Hey, I'm not finished with you," Amanda said. "Did Mitsui send you?"

"What an extraordinary idea," Betty said. "Of course not."

"Denise was, like, real cozy with him. I saw them together lots of times away from the office. Jerry didn't know. Maybe George did. She was always pretending, you know? Her poor sick mother, all the things she gave up. I know from somebody who lives over there that her mother was never sick a day. And she had a boyfriend. I've seen them out places when she didn't know I was there. She had a whole lot of money she didn't earn here. Jerry thinks she was some kind of superwoman, but the rest of us knew. Somebody had enough, if you ask me. I know I did."

Betty understood that Denise hadn't been especially kind to Amanda, but perhaps with good reason. She didn't imagine that this slip of a girl had driven a car into Denise Legrand because she'd bossed her around. Yet Betty suspected that in an odd way Denise Legrand had been as much a role model for Amanda as she had been for young Eve.

"Jerry was scared of her. Nicole didn't trust her."

"His wife. Yes."

Amanda looked a touch smug. "Of course, Nicole doesn't trust me, either." She was pleased with the idea. "Different reasons, naturally."

"Miss Glyn, I don't really need to know any of this."

"Just as long as you don't think you're going to move into her place, just like that." She didn't actually snap her fingers, but the gesture was implied.

"I've already said I'll be gone soon."

"You're too old, for one thing. Even Denise was too old, only she wouldn't admit it. She tried to act like a young person, but you could see she'd had plastic surgery, and I know she dyed her hair."

Now Betty became mildly annoyed. "Young woman, you have no call to insult the dead," she said sternly.

Amanda appeared unfazed by Betty's annoyance. "I could go a lot further," she said. She raised her voice to an unbecoming shrillness. "I know *all* about Denise and all about what's going on. I could tell a lot of interesting stuff. You'd better be careful. Look what happened to Denise." She was almost shouting as Betty reached the door.

"I don't know what you mean," Betty said. "I'm only a temp."

And thank goodness for that, she thought as she departed from Jerry's office. Perhaps retirement wasn't as grim as it had seemed.

"Ah, Tanya. I was just on my way to find you."

Tanya frowned. She was standing not far from Jerry's office and had surely overheard Amanda's silly outburst. "Trouble with the office flirt already? Come on. You're doing okay on the accounts."

Betty was a bit embarrassed to be pleased that Tanya, so much younger but certainly not wiser, could find little to fault in her work. That was a comedown for the mighty Betty, who was accustomed to having people report to her.

She decided against asking Tanya about exactly what had been going on in the conference room. Tanya already seemed to find her too curious.

Eileen was another story.

"Oh, gee, yes. You sure surprised us." She was poring over *Bride's* magazine when Betty found time later to stop at the reception desk. It appeared that Eileen and her Billy were headed for matrimony complete with a lace garter and a too-expensive reception. "I guess we forgot you were here."

"I thought that if the office was planning to contribute . . . I didn't know her, but . . ."

"Contribute? Oh, you mean like for flowers? Mr. Preston didn't mention that."

"I misunderstood."

Eileen lowered her voice. "Mr. Hammond told us we

should keep quiet about Denise and the company, if anyone asks. Then Jerry said to refer people to him. Mr. Hammond got kinda mad at that and took off. I can't believe anybody killed her on purpose, but Jerry said the police might be asking questions. Billy will kill me if I get mixed up with the police."

"If you have anything to tell them, I advise telling the truth," Betty said. "Death is a serious matter."

Eileen looked scared. "I don't know anything. Amanda . . ."

"Yes? What about her?"

"She's always saying things about Denise. Nobody pays any attention. She's trouble. Always trying to get tight with Jerry and Mr. Hammond. From the way she talks, she probably . . ." Eileen stopped. "It couldn't have been any of us."

"Are there others whom I haven't met?" Betty asked.

"Only Reuben the office boy, and the guys who do programming, but they hardly ever even talked to Denise. They don't even let us go downstairs where they work."

"Ah. So few to do so much."

Betty left Eileen to her visions of reembroidered lace and bridesmaids' shoes dyed to match.

Soon enough the day was over, with Betty in possession of a complicated sort of key from Reuben the office boy to let herself into the building in the morning and no further sight of Amanda.

By the time Betty reached East Moulton around six, her new house had started to seem like a welcome haven. She had accumulated plenty to think about. She had learned almost more than she cared to know about Denise Legrand, but even safely back in East Moulton she was still not yet free of her.

At the frozen-food case at the supermarket, Denise had another opportunity to haunt her. As Betty pondered the prospect of one more frozen dinner from the microwave, she caught a glimpse of the imposing and disapproving

Mrs. Brown sailing along an aisle pushing a loaded shopping cart.

The younger man who picked items off the shelves at her instructions had a lean and engaging face, but he looked solemn and stoic. This was very likely the son who had been "involved" with Denise years ago—and who had found her dead at the side of the road. It wasn't surprising that he looked sad. The bonds of even an old romance tended to linger.

Betty chose her dinner quickly and was checked out before she could come face-to-face with Mrs. Brown and her son.

Betty next saw the denim-jacketed back of the self-styled Eve from the roadside produce stand. She was leaning against a car in the supermarket parking lot, engaged in conversation with a youth whose longish hair indicated that perhaps he wasn't the type of boy Eve's father would approve of. Eve seemed to be pleading with him while he shook his head at regular intervals. She wondered if she should take Eve aside, urge her to tell someone what Betty suspected she'd seen on Friday night. Then she decided that it wasn't her place to interfere, solely because she thought she had detected fear.

The sun was setting behind the trees as Betty sat down to eat her dinner without much enthusiasm. There had to be some decent restaurants in the area. East Moulton was close enough to the shores of Long Island Sound to expect restaurants with fresh seafood. She had once caught a glimpse along the road into East Moulton of a somewhat incongruous spot called Southern and Soul inhabiting a white Victorian gingerbread house complete with gables and spacious porches. And yes, she could spend a little more time on cooking for herself. Healthful, nourishing meals, packed with the right kind of vitamins to keep the years at bay. Her doctor's words again.

The lamppost was lighted at the end of the Saks driveway, but Edward Kelso's house was dark behind the pines and maples.

It was past twilight but not quite dark when a car slowed down on Timberhill Road and came to a stop across the street. Betty got up to look through the slats of the blinds. It was a blue and white police car.

She immediately thought: It's about Denise Legrand. Molly Perkins said Denise and Kelso were friends. He had been out in his car the night she died. Now Edward Kelso was being visited by the police.

She could make out two men approaching Edward Kelso's door, but she couldn't see whether they were admitted to the house.

Betty let the slat fall back into place and returned to her dinner and "Headline News" on TV, which gave her a slick and simple summary of world events without taxing her with in-depth analysis.

Betty nearly fell from her chair when the doorbell rang. She'd never heard it before, and she surely wasn't expecting to hear it now.

On her doorstep stood a handsome state trooper in uniform. Not too young, very serious, and not anyone she was expecting to see.

"Miss . . . Trenka?" He looked at a notebook he carried.

"Yes. Elizabeth Trenka. I just moved here. How on earth . . .?"

The state trooper managed a slight smile. "We have our ways, ma'am. Please don't be alarmed. We are trying to locate Mr. Ted Kelso across the street. I understood he was housebound, but he doesn't appear to be in. I wondered if you'd seen him lately."

"I haven't ever seen him," Betty said. "I don't know him. I really have just moved in, only last week. But I think you're mistaken about him being confined to his house. I've seen a car drive in and the lights go on, so he does get about."

"I see. When was that?"

She regretted having mentioned Mr. Kelso's ventures out of the house, so she decided to play dumb on that question. "From time to time. I don't exactly remember. Is there anything wrong?" Betty asked cautiously. She didn't imagine that he'd blurt out anything important.

"We need to speak to him," the state trooper said. "Please don't concern yourself."

Betty decided to concern herself. "Is it about Denise Legrand?"

The trooper quickly suppressed a look of suspicion. "It's police business," he said. Then he added, "Did you know her?"

"Not at all," Betty said quickly. She had talked herself into this corner, so she'd better finish it. "I never met her. I'm working as temporary office help at the place where she worked and naturally the girls were talking . . ."

"Working there, but you didn't meet her." He was looking at her speculatively, perhaps wondering what had become of all the cute young typists who were supposed to do temp work.

"I started today," Betty said. "It was arranged last Friday. Actually, Denise suggested my name to the president." Then she realized how odd that sounded. A dead woman recommending someone she didn't know, who didn't know her. "I put up a notice about work on the supermarket bulletin board. She saw it. I'm sorry, would you care to come in?"

"No," the trooper said. "I think that's all."

Betty didn't think that was all. "Was she killed on purpose?" she asked, figuring that it didn't much matter now if she kept her curiosity to herself.

"Why would you think that?" The trooper was wary.

"I had a picture in my mind of a deer caught in the headlights, and I thought how unlikely hit-and-run was." She thought of poor uneasy Eve at her produce stand. "I wonder if someone right there at the time could actually have seen what happened."

"Mmm," the trooper said. "A neighbor with insomnia merely saw a car from her window late at night. Thanks for your help."

Betty watched him consult with the other trooper in the police car and then they drove off.

She found it hard to concentrate on the latest global messes, the sports scores, the weather, and the state of the economy as purveyed by Ted Turner's people. Should she have mentioned her suspicions about Eve? That look of fear she'd had when Betty talked about someone witnessing Denise's death.

"I'll mind my own business," Betty said aloud to her empty house, then shook her head. Talking to oneself was not a good sign. Perhaps if she got herself a cat, one-sided conversations could be justified. She shook her head again. She had no affinity for cats, although she admired dogs. Other people's.

Betty went upstairs to change from her working clothes into a comfortable patchwork skirt and a loose shirt in natural-colored cotton. The bigger of the two bedrooms, the one she'd made her own, faced the street. Here she'd used curtains left over from her old apartment. Eventually she'd find some that were a better fit for the room.

It was her custom to plan her next day's clothes the night before, in case she overslept. She never had, but the habit was not easily broken after all these years. She pondered the advisability of a sober black or a navy blue as appropriate under the circumstances of death at Zig-Zag. She took her nice navy dress with the silver buttons at the neck and cuffs from the closet and was hanging it over the door when she saw the lights of a car coming from the direction of town. She saw the car slow down and then turn into Edward Kelso's driveway.

She stood at the window, thinking. What was a good neighbor? Should she tell Edward Kelso that the police were seeking to speak with him? Jerry Preston's summons to cooperate with the police indicated that all was not quite right about Denise's death. The almost secret meeting in the conference room suggested a degree of concern beyond mere real or feigned grief for their colleague.

What was the definition of a nosy old woman who wanted to find out what was what?

Betty had to laugh at herself. She was trying to be all things to all people—in other words, a good but nosy neighbor. She wouldn't try to telephone him. Instead she took a big red-orange shawl from a drawer to protect herself against the evening chill, slung it around her shoulders, and marched out into the night, across the street.

CHAPTER 8

RIGHT BEFORE Betty rang Edward Kelso's doorbell, she almost turned to go back home. She didn't know what to expect. A frail man, older than she, perhaps, living alone (or Penny Saks would have told her otherwise). Reclusive and suffering from some chronic debilitating illness. He might rightly be enraged at her intrusion.

Well, she'd faced enraged men before and had come out of it comparatively unscathed, largely because she had remained calm in the face of unleashed emotions that were often quite irrational. Men, she had learned, now and then spoke and acted before they thought of the consequences. This moment might be embarrassing, but it could be nothing compared with certain significantly bad ones she'd survived in the past. She rang the bell.

There were lights on in the rooms at the back of the house, although the front room was dark.

She rang again, now prepared to leave quietly after half a minute's wait. There were limits to both neighborliness and curiosity.

A disembodied voice distorted by electronics said, "Who is it?" Then, "Push that white button to speak. The one below the doorbell."

She pushed the button. "It's Elizabeth Trenka, your neighbor from across the street."

"This is not convenient," the voice said. "Could we do the good-neighbor bit another time?"

"If you wish," Betty said. "This isn't a getting-to-know-you call. It's about the police. And Denise."

Silence.

She'd give him ten seconds this time. The night was chillier than she thought and her shawl was not enough to ward off the cold.

Edward Kelso didn't turn on the lights in the front room before he opened the door. Thus Betty's first view of him gave the sudden impression of a squat, misshapen body, less than four feet tall, backlit by the lights from the room at the back.

"Ah . . . Mr. Kelso?" She remembered later being totally flustered at the sight but managing to speak calmly. Then he reached out and flicked on a light over the steps.

What Betty saw now was a man of apparently normal height and configuration seated in a wheelchair. He was not an old man at all but somewhere in his forties, with graying hair and a trim gray beard. He had sharp, pale eyes, probably blue, but it was hard to tell in this light. His regular but interesting features at this moment expressed a distinct distaste for the sight of the woman on his doorstep.

"What about the police?" he demanded. "What about Denise?"

"They were here this evening looking for you. I understand you are her friend."

Ted Kelso gave her a long look. "Was. She's dead," he said. "Come on in, as long as you're here." He turned his wheelchair and preceded her. "Close that door, will you? I don't want the whole neighborhood in here. Every time I turn around one of those Saks kids is begging to come in to fool around with my computers and video stuff."

Betty followed him as he wheeled his chair toward the back of the house. The floors were of polished wood and uncarpeted, so he moved smoothly on rubber wheels into a large, brightly colored room that seemed a combination of kitchen–dining area, office, study, and living room. It was low and spacious, and even boasted a couple of leather armchairs as well as a computer on a wheeled stand next to a big square table piled with books and papers. One wall was devoted to electronics: television set, VCR, speakers, and various bits of technical equipment Betty couldn't begin to understand. There were racks of CDs and videos and bookcases filled with books.

An elaborate cooktop took up space on one side of the room next to a built-in oven and a double-door refrigerator. The spaces under the sink and the counters puzzled her until she realized that he could move his wheelchair in under them to be close to the work areas. Polished copper pots and pans hung from a ceiling rack attached to a device that appeared capable of lowering them electronically.

It was not a normal room in any sense but was carefully designed to accommodate Edward Kelso's needs entirely.

"Sit," he said.

She took the armchair he indicated, and he brought his chair around to face her.

"What's this about?" He was very nearly glaring at her.

Betty decided that at her age she would not be intimidated by this gruff young man, or his wheelchair. She would be businesslike.

"I don't mean to intrude," she said. "I thought you ought to be informed that the police were here earlier to speak with you."

"Why did you think that? I don't know you, you don't know me. No reason for you to be concerned about my business with the police, whatever it may be."

"Absolutely true," Betty said, "but I do have some interest in the matter of Denise Legrand's death."

He looked at her through narrowed eyes. "Explain that."

"Without knowing me, Denise saw to it that I was hired to take her place for a few days at Zig-Zag. Then she was suddenly killed. There are rumors about the office that someone did it on purpose. Well, one can usually discount ninety-nine percent of that sort of gossip, but the police were on to Mr. Preston. He's the young man who—"

"I know about Jerry Preston," Ted said. "I know about all of them. Exactly why did you decide to come here?"

"The police came around to you. They rang my bell when you weren't home. Mr. Kelso, I thought . . ." He sat waiting for her to speak, but she sensed his impatience: the hands that gripped the arms of his chair; the way he hunched his shoulders, then relaxed them when she said, "I've come to believe that it wasn't an unfortunate hit-and-run accident."

"It wasn't," he said grimly. "It was murder." He spoke with absolute certainty. Betty felt a pang of anxiety. He might be confined to a wheelchair, but he certainly got about readily in his car. She'd seen him come and go.

"I understand," she said casually, "that the police nowadays are able to determine all sorts of things about whether a particular car might have hit something. I mean, once they find the car, there are tests for paint flecks and dents—"

If Betty had been startled by the sight of him in his doorway, she was entirely confused by his reaction now.

Ted Kelso put back his head and laughed out loud.

"Am I so amusing, Mr. Kelso?" Betty asked crossly, but she wondered if his response indicated mental instability. Murder, to her mind, was not an occasion for merriment.

He caught his breath. "I apologize. Denise was an old friend. She was very good to me and I don't take her death lightly." He was serious again. "It was just the idea of our neighborhood granny ferreting out if I am a murderer."

Now Betty was amused, but only very slightly. "Hardly a neighborhood granny, Mr. Kelso, but—"

"But you can't be too careful. I'm sorry . . . Mrs. . . . Miss Trenka? A Czech name, isn't it?"

"So few people recognize its origin," she said. "And Miss Trenka will do fine."

"I haven't had the heart to laugh since I heard about Denise. I saw her on Friday, the night she died—much earlier in the evening. We went out to dinner."

"Did she say anything to indicate that she was in danger? Do you have any suspicions?"

Ted Kelso raised his hand to stop the questions. "That is my business, Miss Trenka. And the police, if I choose to tell them." He hesitated, and she thought he did have something to share. All he said was, "Denise was very up at dinner. Business was going well, she was looking forward to New York. That's it. I do appreciate your concern in wanting me to know about the police, but I have some work to attend to, so I'd be just as happy if you'd run along to your knitting."

Betty stood up. "I don't knit, Mr. Kelso. Never have, never will. Not only am I not the neighborhood granny, I'm not the nosy neighborhood spinster hot on the trail of criminals."

"No." He surveyed her thoughtfully. "I suppose you're not. You said you were stepping in for Denise at Zig-Zag?"

"Not really. I retired recently," Betty said, "not by my choice, I assure you." Even she could hear the submerged resentment in her voice and tried to bury it deeper. "I needed something temporary to fill in while I decide what to do. I haven't begun to examine my choices."

"You have nothing to be so angry about. These things happen. You're still in a position to have plenty of choices."

She couldn't tell if there was bitterness behind his words or whether it was just the gruffness that seemed to come naturally from him.

"I'm quite happy," Betty said. "I am *not* angry. Not at all."

"Clearly untrue, but never mind," he said. He surveyed her for a long moment. Betty felt uncomfortable under his scrutiny. He was a man quite a bit younger than she, to be sure, but he certainly would be considered attractive. He had a sort of commanding presence in spite of his disability. "Look, Miss Trenka, I wonder . . ." He started to move himself toward the front of the house to show her out. "Never mind."

Betty stood still. "Is there something I can do for you?"

Ted Kelso looked back over his shoulder. "In the long, short, or middle run?"

"Whatever."

"Long run, my problems are not readily solvable. Middle

run, I can handle everything"—he gestured around his living area—"probably more efficiently than you can."

"That's the truth," Betty said. "There's no limit to the things I can't do around the house. What about the short run?"

"How long will you be at Zig-Zag?"

"For a couple more days. It could conceivably stretch out through the week, given everything that's happened. I have no intention of staying on beyond that."

"I see. I'd like to know what's really going on over there."

"Would you? So would I, but I'm not in anyone's confidence, Mr. Kelso."

He leaned his forearms on the arms of his wheelchair. "Look, call me Ted, okay? And I've changed my mind about throwing you out. I cared about Denise, and her death was a real blow. I'm sure she was up to something at Zig-Zag, but she didn't confide in me. She's been hinting over the past couple months."

"What kind of hints?"

Ted shook his head. "Nothing specific. Changes coming. More money, I know it had to do with money. Power. Being in control. No more orders to be obeyed."

"Nothing more specific?" She frowned.

"You sound disappointed."

"It sounds like the fantasy a lot of women in business have."

He looked at her questioningly. "My dear Miss Trenka, surely you didn't fantasize along those lines."

She shrugged. "Of course I did, but my reality was different. You knew Denise a long time then?"

"Yes," he said. "From before."

Betty understood that he meant before what had happened to him had happened. She didn't wish to hear what it was, not just now.

"Now that you're brought up the issue of dreams and reality, I wish I knew . . ." He hesitated. "There are things I can't do for myself in this situation, even if I didn't have this." He patted the arm of the wheelchair. "I can't walk into Zig-Zag and corner Jerry Preston. I could use your help." His smile was charming and ingratiating. Betty was sure it had helped him get his way many times. She'd personally never cared much for beards, but Ted Kelso's looked quite distinguished.

"I can repeat the idle office gossip right now," she said. "Denise wasn't especially popular with the girls, although the receptionist admired her clothes. A snip of a girl named Amanda Glyn has designs on the boss." She stopped. "And designs on Denise's job, I should add. According to George Hammond, who seems to have some influence, a Mr. Mitsui is rumored to have reached these shores, much to everyone's surprise."

Ted looked at her. "Mitsui is definitely someone to consider," he said. "What is being said about him?"

"I know nothing except he's been negotiating with Zig-Zag on some business matter. Denise worked well with him. There's nothing more I can tell you and little more I can discover. I ought to be going." She didn't want to get herself further involved with Zig-Zag simply to help Ted Kelso ease his obvious sorrow over his friend's death.

"I need to know more, dammit," he said almost angrily as she made a move to leave. "I know she was handling negotiations with Mitsui, but there was more to it than the software Preston already has on the market. I need to know."

"I'm sure you're accustomed to getting your own way, but I can't be manipulated so easily," Betty said. She decided she could reach the front door ahead of him and be gone before he could stop her with words.

"Denise was going to meet Mitsui in New York this weekend," Ted said to her back. "Her death put a stop to that. Doesn't that interest you?"

"Coincidence," Betty said at the door. It stopped her.

"Murder," Ted said.

"There's surely no connection. He was in New York . . ."

"A lot of people weren't. They were right here in East

Moulton," he said. "Listen to this. When I dropped her off after dinner, she said she had to make some calls. She wanted them out of the way before she went off early Saturday morning. Who did she call? Why was she out in the middle of the night?"

"She was taking a walk."

Ted shook his head. "Never. Denise wouldn't dream of taking a walk alone in the dark. Damn." He frowned and was silent.

"Mr. Kelso? Ted?"

"Stupid how you react to the unthinkable," he said. "She was going to pick up a couple of things for me in the city. I'm suddenly worried about some books and a springform baking pan from Peter Bridge, and Denise is dead."

Betty was struck by the look of sadness on his face. "Even if I wanted to, I surely couldn't find out what she was up to, as you put it," she said. "I'm not in—what do they say?—the loop. It's out of the question anyhow. I don't care to be your spy."

"Couldn't you think of it as working for justice?" he asked. There was that ingratiating smile again.

She thought, I am too old to be swayed by a good-looking young man. "Exactly what is it you want?"

"Anything out of the ordinary. The way they react. Something more than the usual upset over a co-worker's sudden death."

Betty gave in, a little. "They had some kind of closed-door meeting in the conference room today. I wasn't asked, but I accidentally walked in on them. They were more than startled. Frightened, but not, I think, by me. I don't know exactly what Mr. Preston had been saying to them. Or this George Hammond, a fairly awful man. Is he the Hammond in Hammond Center?"

Ted chuckled. "That and more. He's Jerry Preston's father-in-law."

"Ahh ... The money behind Zig-Zag. I see. All I could get from the receptionist was that they were told not to talk about it. Mr. Preston was summoned to see the police. What is it?"

Ted was gazing intently at a distant spot. "Nothing. But the police also want to see me. And I was among the last to see her alive. Do me a favor. No spying, but watch and listen."

As Betty pondered whether to agree, the telephone rang. Ted Kelso reached out and picked up the receiver. It was a cordless phone like hers, easy to carry about the room.

"Yes," he said to the caller. "I'm at home. I had an appointment earlier. Yes, I'll be here if you come in half an hour." He hung up. "Bustle on home, Miss Trenka. The cops are on their way and you wouldn't want to be caught conniving with a suspect."

"You could easily be a suspect," she said, "since you were with her that night. And by the way, I'd prefer to be called Elizabeth."

"All right, Elizabeth. Do you eat?"

"Regularly."

"I meant, do you like to eat good food? If you do, I'll feed you. Come around seven tomorrow and tell me what you've seen and heard."

"How . . . how nice." Anything was better than another frozen dinner.

"Not nice so much as the fact that cooking for two is more interesting than cooking for one."

"Is there anything—" she began, but he interrupted.

"Oh, God, please don't suggest bringing something," he said. "No sour cream dip, no cake baked from a package. Trust me. Now move, or you're going to get caught up with the resident state policeman."

Betty paused at the door. "Will you be going to Denise's funeral tomorrow?"

"I'm not sure," he said. "I'm not good at occasions that command the presence of large numbers of people. Not," he added quickly, "because of my disability. I never cared for crowds or shared tears."

"Until tomorrow evening then," she said. "The entire office except me has been instructed to be at the funeral, so I'll be at the office alone until they come back. Mr. Preston asked me to handle things."

"I have no trouble believing that's well within your capabilities."

Betty opened the door and looked back at Ted Kelso in his wheelchair. "I don't suppose you have any idea who killed Denise."

"It wasn't me," he said. "More than that I am not willing to say."

"I went by the place on Prospect Street where it happened," Betty said. "It didn't look to me as though a car had been involved at all."

Betty recrossed Timberhill Road, fully aware that she had been manipulated after all. Not only that, she was more certain than ever that Denise's death had not been accidental.

CHAPTER 9

THE PARKING lot of Zig-Zag was empty of cars when Betty arrived at quarter to nine the next morning. The day was cloudy, with rain forecast for later in the day.

Betty used the complicated-looking key to unlock the front door—having sworn to return it to Reuben the office boy the moment she saw him. Reuben had stroked his not yet successful mustache and seemed reluctant to give up his "mister key," as he called it. Jerry had insisted, so he had taken it off his key ring and handed it to her. She followed his unlocking instructions with only a little difficulty and then pushed. The door opened easily, and she wondered if it had already been unlocked.

She wasn't alarmed, however, since she had half expected Jerry Preston to stop in before the funeral. Under similar circumstances Sid Senior would certainly have managed to come to the Edwards & Son offices first. Sid Junior was another story.

No one was about when she entered the reception area and found the main switch to turn on the overhead fluorescent lights. She walked down the corridor to Jerry Preston's office and peered in, but it was dark and empty.

In the copier room she examined the on-off switch for the thermostat and fan control. She turned the fan on and heard a hum as air began to circulate throughout the building. The coffeemaker stood clean and empty. She decided to take it upon herself to make coffee for those who would arrive later. For herself she'd stopped and bought coffee at the doughnut shop in the minimall that seemed to constitute

Hammond Center. Alone in the Zig-Zag offices, she felt a familiar sense of belonging, although she didn't pretend that it was anything more than a momentary step back into her past.

She was glad that Ted Kelso hadn't asked her to pry through Zig-Zag's files or anything of that nature. Her ingrained principles of privacy would have forced her to refuse. Listening was something else.

Back in the reception area she looked out through the main glass door. A sudden spattering of rain had dampened the tarmac on the drive in front of the building. It struck her suddenly that she was quite alone in a big building rather far from the others in the office park. She locked the door from the inside and hoped there weren't other ways into the building.

For the next half hour Betty sat quietly at the reception desk, ready for phone calls that didn't come, and leafed through a book she'd brought with her about travel to the Far East. Hong Kong sounded interesting; she had doubts about Thailand. India seemed almost too overwhelming. The expense was considerable, so even with her Edwards & Son money, it wasn't likely that she'd get that far. There was always a tour of Europe, perhaps one that would take her to her grandfather's homeland.

Her thoughts came around briefly to Edward Kelso and her assignment at Zig-Zag for him. How interesting that he had recognized her name as Czech. She wondered exactly what he did. Work at something at home? Penny Saks hadn't indicated that he went out to work. A scholar, perhaps, or a writer . . .

The sound of muffled pounding on the door brought her back to the mundane world of word processing and hanging folders. A small woman in a dark tailored suit, short dark hair, and a ferocious scowl was hammering away at the glass to get Betty's attention.

As Betty fumbled to unlock the door, the woman stood outside with her hands on her hips glaring at her. An expensive-looking black car was idling in the drive in front of the building, its driver's door open as though the woman was in too great a rush to close it behind her.

"I locked it," Betty said. "So sorry ... here alone ..."

The woman pushed past her.

"Where is he?"

"There's no one here but me. Are you all right?"

The woman was shaking, apparently from rage. She turned on Betty. "Idiot! I'm talking about my husband. Is he here?"

"Mrs. Preston?" Betty asked cautiously. Executives' wives were not her favorite people. The only thing worse, perhaps, were executives' mistresses, if Sid Junior's attachments were any example. Then she remembered that this was George Hammond's daughter and decided that extreme politeness was in order. "Can I assist you?"

"He was supposed to drive me to the funeral for that damned woman, but he was gone before I got up, and he didn't come back for me. I had to drive myself." She seemed outraged at the idea. Betty thought that black car looked quite comfortable.

"He wasn't here when I arrived, Mrs. Preston."

"Well, had he been here? Did you look in his office?"

"No, I didn't think to."

"Then I'll look. Nobody else around? The programmers?"

"I wouldn't know. The door's locked. No admittance."

"Never mind. He couldn't have been here all night." Mrs. Preston—Nicole, if Betty remembered correctly— marched down the hall and flung open the door to Jerry's office. Betty followed her to the head of the corridor and saw her step inside for a moment. Then she came out pulling the door shut with a slam. Betty retreated to her post at the receptionist's desk. No point in irritating Nicole Preston further with the idea that she was being watched.

A moment later Nicole stopped abruptly at the desk to look Betty over. "You're the new one, are you? More of Denise's handiwork. At least you're not an aspiring femme fatale. I'll thank you not to tell anyone that I was here."

Nicole Preston departed without another word, kind or otherwise.

Finally, after a long silence, the phone rang.

"Zig-Zag, good morning."

Panic lay ill concealed behind Jerry Preston's words. "Has my wife been there?"

Betty hesitated. Nicole had commanded her not to tell anyone. Then she decided she didn't take orders from Nicole Preston, who had been unnecessarily rude to her in any case. "She left fifteen minutes ago. She seemed . . . somewhat upset."

"What did she say? I mean, I went home to change clothes for the funeral and pick her up, but she was gone. The nanny thought she was still in bed, but she had left."

"I'd treat her gently, if I were you," Betty said. Then she added, "If you don't mind me mentioning it."

"That bad, huh? I . . . I went out pretty early to jog and forgot the time." Jerry Preston was making an ineffective and unnecessary attempt at explaining. Betty didn't care to know. "Nothing to be done about it now," he said. "I'll be in after the service. If a guy named Mitsui calls . . . I forgot. You know the name. If Mitsui calls, tell him I won't be in until much later. Meetings—you know what to say. I need more time."

Betty sighed. Even two more days at Zig-Zag were beginning to sound too long, however much Ted Kelso wanted to know about the company.

She found her place in her book. She'd read only a few pages when she stopped. She didn't move, didn't look up, but she knew that someone had come into the building very quietly and was now standing in front of her desk. She hadn't relocked the door when Nicole Preston left. She pretended to continue reading, hoping that the person would speak. She hoped she was bigger or stronger or faster if it was someone threatening. And the door for a possible escape wasn't far from where she sat.

"Mr. Preston."

She looked up, relieved, at the sound of the polite voice.

"Ah." Now she stood up and faced the Japanese man on the other side of the reception desk. He was of medium height, with a plumpish, round face, which at the moment was entirely expressionless. His hair was thick and black, and he wore a very correct dark gray suit and a black tie with a faint gray stripe. He held his hat in one hand.

"Mr. Mitsui, I presume. I am Elizabeth Trenka, in charge here for the moment."

He bowed. She felt she was towering over him, but she towered over many men, except for National Basketball Association players.

"Mr. Preston?" This time it was a question.

"I'm afraid he's out of the office. I was not told to expect you." She saw through the main glass door the long black limousine with smoked-glass windows that had evidently brought him.

"He did not know that I was coming here," Mr. Mitsui said. He spoke carefully in almost unaccented English, but there was a hint of someone consciously striving to utter correctly the difficult combinations of consonants and vowels of a foreign language. He looked around with some curiosity. "Miss Legrand?"

"I'm afraid . . . That is, Miss Legrand is dead."

"Ah." Mr. Mitsui's face rearranged itself imperceptibly to indicate grave seriousness. "How did this happen? I knew Miss Legrand. I had an appointment to see her in New York, but she failed to appear." In spite of the fact that there was an obvious reason why Denise had not kept her appointment, Mr. Mitsui now managed to convey by his expression that he was extremely put out.

"It was a terrible accident," Betty said.

Now Mr. Mitsui invoked the name of George Hammond.

"I'm very much afraid that everyone is attending Miss Legrand's funeral this morning," she said. "Perhaps you'd care to wait, but it may be some time. The funeral is at ten and it's just that now."

Mr. Mitsui pondered. Betty assumed he understood what she had said, although the small frown on his face suggested that he might be carefully translating her words into Japanese.

I can deal with this, Betty thought, if only I knew where the correct place was to store him until Jerry arrives.

"The conference room is quite comfortable," she said, relieved to have thought of the perfect spot. For all she knew, Mitsui was the head of some vast, powerful conglomerate that sought to acquire Jerry Preston's company and his software for untold millions and was thus not to be offended in any way.

Mr. Mitsui turned on his heel and walked to the main door. He signaled to someone outside and in a moment a uniformed chauffeur—young, American, and incurious— appeared with a briefcase that he handed in through the door.

"One hour," Mr. Mitsui said after examining his watch. The driver nodded and departed. Within seconds the limousine headed around toward the parking area.

"I will wait in the conference room," Mr. Mitsui said. "There is a telephone?"

"Why, yes. I believe so. I'm quite new with the company and don't—"

Mr. Mitsui did not seem interested in her employment history. He waited, hat and briefcase in hand, for Betty to lead the way.

"This way," she said, and proceeded down the corridor and trusted him to follow.

Although she was certain that Nicole Preston had slammed shut the door of Jerry's office, it was ajar now. Betty closed it gently as they passed.

"Would you like coffee? Tea?"

Mr. Mitsui took one of the large comfortable chairs on the side of the long table near the telephone. "It is not necessary." He waved her away. He might have been overcome by the strain of speaking correct English, but more likely he had no further use for the company of a low-level Zig-Zag employee.

"I'll just be out in front then, if you need anything."

Mr. Mitsui took a compact electronic device from his briefcase and punched in a series of numbers. Then he reached for the telephone. Betty left him to it.

In the next quiet half hour, interrupted only by a handful of incoming calls, Betty noted that Mr. Mitsui was on the line almost continuously. At least he was occupied and didn't expect her to entertain him, a feat she believed was beyond her. She had read a good deal in the papers about the impact of Japanese business on America, had seen television interviews with Japanese businessmen and politicians, but she had had no direct dealings with the Japanese. More power to Denise if, as Jerry had said, she'd understood them. Betty had personal memories that the comparative youngsters at Zig-Zag couldn't share: a great war that had come upon her world as she approached her early teens. The war had stayed around a long time. The Japanese of those years were not friends, and old memories die hard.

Betty dragged herself back to the present and noticed that the light that had indicated that Mr. Mitsui was using the telephone had gone dark. Under such circumstances in her old job she would have asked if she could provide anything to an important office visitor.

Well, why not?

She went along the corridor toward the conference room and stopped short at Jerry Preston's office door. It was open again and the lights were on. She stepped cautiously into the office. The door to Denise's connecting office was open as well, and she was startled to see Mr. Mitsui standing in the doorway, his hands behind his back.

For an instant she was deeply offended that he would dare to enter a private office but held back from speaking. There was something odd. Mr. Mitsui's head was bowed slightly as though he was staring at the floor beyond Denise's desk.

"Excuse me," Betty said, but Mr. Mitsui did not turn.

Instead, he raised his head and stared out the window at the damp lawns and dripping laurel bushes. "There is a problem here," he said to the window. "I am very sorry that you find me here." He turned to face her. "I cannot be involved." He brushed past her and left through Jerry's office.

"What . . . what were you doing here? Wait!" Betty called after him, but he kept going.

She hurried into Denise's office to see what Mr. Mitsui's problem was.

Amanda Glyn was sprawled on the floor in the midst of potting soil and broken shards from one of the big pottery plants that stood on the table in front of the window. Blood was clotted in her ringlets and had seeped out onto the light-colored rug. It had soaked into the front of the white blouse she wore under her dark blue jacket and was already nearly dry. The plant—a large one with tangled roots—lay beside her. The desk chair had fallen over.

Betty knelt beside her and felt for a pulse in her neck and wrist but could detect none. Her skin was cold. She allowed herself ten seconds of rapid thought. There was no possibility that Amanda was alive, no chance that CPR would revive her, keep her life going on a thin thread until help came.

Amanda's eyes were open, staring at nothing. Betty tried to brush aside the idea that there was a look of fear or surprise that death had frozen in them.

If I mess about too much, Betty thought, I could destroy the important evidence people are always talking about.

Mr. Mitsui had been on his own at the end of the corridor for some time—time enough to kill Amanda, although the possibility seemed farfetched.

She jerked her head up and listened. Was he still in the building, ready to kill again? Then she realized how ridiculous that was. Mr. Mitsui had shown no signs of being involved in a struggle, and surely Amanda had been dead for longer than that, longer even than Nicole Preston's appearance on the scene.

She felt again for a pulse and then lifted the receiver on Denise's desk and dialed 911, hoping that the number would reach an emergency operator. As the phone rang once, twice, she whispered, "Have mercy on the soul of Thy departed servant. . . ."

"There's been an accident," she said to the emergency operator who came on the line.

That was inaccurate.

Amanda had not been accidentally smashed by the heavy ceramic planter.

Human hands had held the large blue and yellow urn and had intentionally smashed Amanda as she sat in the chair behind Denise Legrand's desk.

CHAPTER 10

So YOUNG to be dead, Betty thought to herself not for the first time since the police and the emergency people had arrived, and what were Amanda Glyn's sins? Ambition and bad manners. Bad temper. Not serious sins in the accepted sense. She thought back to her conversation with Amanda, such as it had been. Amanda had implied a knowledge of matters others might prefer to keep secret. If she had been so ready to hint this to a stranger like Betty, she might also have been equally free with her hints to others. Not very wise, but she thought wisdom was something Amanda Glyn hadn't managed to acquire.

She saw the ambulance men wheel out a collapsible stretcher with the body zipped into a dark green bag. The volunteer firemen who had also responded to her emergency call milled about in the reception area. Her acquaintance of the previous night, the state trooper, was speaking on the phone while another official-looking gentleman in civilian clothes conferred with a doctor. Men from the state police major-crime squad had come quickly with bags and cameras and the like and were still in Denise's office.

Beyond answering a few inane questions, namely who had killed the young woman and had *she* killed the young woman, Betty was left alone. Her responses—"I don't know" and "No, I only met her yesterday"—had satisfied them for the moment. She volunteered nothing. No Mr. Mitsui, no Nicole Preston, no talk of secrets Amanda might have held. No business negotiations.

Betty waited where she was told to wait, on a couch in

the reception area, and pondered some serious questions: Who had killed Amanda, what had become of Mr. Mitsui, and was there any connection between Amanda's death and Denise's?

After calling the emergency forces, she had boldly marched through the building looking into all of the rooms. Mr. Mitsui had not been lurking behind the copier or cowering guiltily in one of the empty offices. The door to the programmer's area remained locked. He must have escaped through the front door and been swept off in his limo.

The phone, which had been silent most of the morning, started to ring.

"Could I take this call?" Betty said to one of the official men hovering around the desk. The phone rang several times before they shrugged and allowed her to pick up the receiver.

"Zig-Zag, good morning." It no longer felt especially good to her. "Ah, Mr. Preston. Yes, I know the phone ought to be answered promptly. I . . ." She looked at her trooper. "I think someone here wishes to speak to you, Mr. Preston." She held out the receiver and the state trooper took it, saving her the trouble of explaining about Amanda and the presence of the police.

"Please sit over there, ma'am," the trooper said. "One of our people will handle the phones." He turned his back on her as he spoke to Jerry.

She was no longer interested in reading about the shops at the Peninsula Hotel in Hong Kong and the Emerald Buddha and the Golden Stupa in Bangkok, but she fixed her eyes on a page so that she could think more about Mr. Mitsui. Although he could not have killed Amanda just before she saw him in Denise's office, what had compelled him to go into that office in the first place? He might have known it was Jerry's—and Denise's—if he'd been here before. He might simply be nosy. She did not think that she could avoid telling the police at least that he had been there this morning. On the other hand, although she had only worked a day at Zig-Zag, she felt an obligation to the company. Mr. Mitsui was involved in whatever was going on with the business. He was to be treated with care. She would be cautious about what she said.

Still, Mr. Mitsui was eventually going to be involved in the murder investigation, whether or not he wanted to be.

And so, too, would Nicole Preston.

She thought about Jerry Preston. According to both him and his wife, he had been abroad early. She knew nothing about him really, nor about his relationship with Amanda except for what Amanda had implied. Could he have been here at Zig-Zag at dawn for a rendezvous with her? One that had ended in violence?

Could he have gone home and confessed to his wife about this horrible event, and had she then come here to see whether Amanda was actually dead? Possible. Nicole Preston seemed to display a certain kind of no-nonsense boldness.

Yet just about anyone could have been here before Betty arrived at eight-forty-five. Anyone at all. Just as anyone could have been driving through the darkness on Prospect Street when Denise was killed.

Two deaths among Zig-Zag's employees. It was a rather dramatic way to reduce the payroll.

Betty looked up as the phone rang again.

"I need to talk to you, Miss Trenka," her trooper said.

"I really should be handling the phones. It isn't fair to the company to have them answered by . . . your people."

"My people will do just fine," he said reluctantly. "I want to ask my questions before the others get here. We've asked them not to go on to the burial."

That didn't seem fair either, but there was nothing to be done. Denise Legrand would wend her way to her final rest without the support of her professional colleagues. She hoped that Ted Kelso would be there, and perhaps Molly Perkins. Even Mrs. Brown's son, Alan, who had shared some interlude with Denise long ago.

"Miss Trenka," the trooper said. "Are you with me? Good. Now explain this morning."

Betty explained: her early arrival, with no evidence that anyone had been there before her, no hint that Amanda was lying dead in Denise's office.

"It was quiet," she said. "Mrs. Preston came by to meet Mr. Preston for the funeral." There, she'd gotten it out. "There'd been some mixup. He wasn't here. She looked about but wasn't out of my sight for more than a few seconds."

"Had he been here at all?"

Betty didn't care for his tone. "Not to my knowledge. I arrived at a quarter to nine."

She saw in her mind's eye Nicole Preston down the corridor opening Jerry's door, but in the mere seconds before she returned to the reception area she could not have killed Amanda.

"I wonder how long she'd been dead," Betty asked then, half rhetorically. She didn't think the police shared that kind of information, but she wanted to know if either Nicole Preston or Mr. Mitsui could conceivably have been the perpetrator.

"Some hours," he said shortly, to her relief. "Possibly it happened late last night or in the early morning hours. Or it might have been right after the end of the business day, after all of you had gone home."

"Oh, certainly not," Betty said.

The trooper gazed at her, waiting to hear more.

"I mean, she wasn't wearing the same clothes when I found her. She had on proper funeral-going clothes . . ." Well, in a sense. The white blouse under her blue jacket was a clinging satiny fabric, rather low-cut for a funeral. "What she was wearing was nothing like what she had on yesterday. *Quite* different. A little blue suit and a white blouse. Wait! She was wearing sneakers. Those fancy things for running the girls wear nowadays, with colored stripes and thick soles. She must have walked here from Hammond Center. There were no cars in the parking lot. . . ."

"I see." He seemed moderately interested. "Anything else?"

Mr. Mitsui, she thought, you're about to become involved.

"There was one other visitor to the office besides Mrs. Preston," Betty said carefully. "A Japanese gentleman to see Mr. Preston. He waited a time and then . . . then he left. Mr. Mitsui. He was not communicative."

"Now explain how you happened to find Miss Glyn."

Betty frowned, concentrating on the implications of distorting the truth slightly until she had a chance to speak to Jerry Preston. No one except she and Mr. Mitsui knew exactly how the body had been discovered. Again, Mr. Mitsui might well have already known Amanda was lying there dead, but it was difficult to construct a plausible scenario that would bring him to Zig-Zag very early in the morning to meet a young woman barely out of her teens and of no particular standing. It was, indeed, far easier to imagine that Mr. Mitsui might have a reason to see Denise Legrand dead, but he had seemed genuinely surprised at the news of her death.

"It's all so confusing," she said finally. She decided to take momentary advantage of her advancing years. "My memory isn't what it was. . . ." That was partly true, but actually what she had trouble remembering were the names of acquaintances from a dozen years ago or movie stars from her youth. The trooper, however, seemed to find the memory lapses of an older lady quite believable. "Let me think. Mr. Mitsui was leaving. I went down the hall toward the conference room where he'd been telephoning . . ." Still fairly true. "The door to Mr. Preston's office was open and the lights were on. I stepped in and saw Miss Glyn lying on the floor of the adjoining office. Miss Legrand's office, that is. I knew immediately that she was dead—"

"How was that?" Spoken sharply.

"I felt for a pulse. She was cold and her eyes were open, staring. The blood on her blouse was dry. It was terrible. I considered attempting CPR but felt there was no point, so I called for help. You came."

"No previous knowledge of her before coming to work here?"

"I told you that I met her only yesterday. And I told you last evening that I am a very recent arrival in this area."

"You also told me that you didn't know Ted Kelso," he said, "but from my conversation with him last night, it appears that he does know you."

"He does know me now," Betty said airily. "Small-town people are so easy to get to know."

"Mmm. Know anything about what this company does?"

"Software. What kind I don't know." She almost chuckled. "To tell the truth, I don't understand software, any more than I understand the telephone. I use them both."

He was not amused, but Betty was saved from further talk by the blustering arrival of George Hammond, red-faced and in a temper. He collared the state trooper immediately.

"What's going on? I got a call at home from one of the guys at the town hall saying there was trouble here."

"Not so fast," the trooper said. "Name?"

"George Hammond. Your people know me. I'm one of the principals of this firm. What kind of trouble? Has that jackass Preston done something illegal?" Hammond glanced at Betty as though he had never seen her before. "Who the hell are you?"

"Betty Trenka. We met . . . saw each other yesterday."

His response was directed to the trooper. "I demand to know . . ." He looked around. "Where is everybody?"

"They're all at Miss Legrand's funeral," Betty said, and was rewarded with unfriendly looks from both Hammond and the trooper. George Hammond had apparently felt no need to bid Denise a final farewell.

"Can we talk somewhere?" the trooper asked.

"Conference room. We won't be in anyone's way." Hammond scowled at Betty. "No calls. Tell Preston to get in there as soon as he gets here. And let me know the minute Mitsui arrives."

Betty didn't have a chance to tell him that Mr. Mitsui had already come and gone.

Hammond and the trooper started toward the conference room. "Okay, what kind of problem? I have a right to know."

"How well did you know Amanda Glyn?" the trooper asked.

Hammond said something softly that Betty couldn't hear. The trooper smiled. Poor Amanda's more obvious characteristics were no doubt most of what George Hammond knew of her. The two men left Betty alone in the reception area, free to consider Mr. Mitsui and the question of who might have killed Amanda and Denise.

She answered the ringing phone, but without the heart for any further "Good mornings."

"Is this the old lady who was in the office this morning?" The male voice was entirely unknown to her.

"Yes," Betty said cautiously. "Who is speaking?"

"Hang on."

The next voice was unmistakably Mr. Mitsui's.

"Please not to tell the authorities of my presence this morning," he said.

"I'm afraid it's too late for that," Betty said. "I cannot lie in a case of murder. But," she added hastily, "I merely said that you had waited for Mr. Preston and had left. The police did not seem especially interested. I did not indicate that you had found the body while prying in the company's private offices."

"Ah." There was a long silence on his end of the line.

"I cannot promise that I will not be asked further questions, and I may have to explain in detail how the scene looked, including your presence. However, I am awaiting the opportunity to speak to Mr. Preston first."

"Thank you, Miss Trenka." It was only later that she realized he had retained her name from their brief encounter. "I will see that you do not find yourself in difficulties with the police, but I must handle matters in my own way, after I have consulted with ... with my superiors."

He hung up abruptly.

The next call was from Nicole Preston. "Is he there yet?"

"Mr. Preston? No. Didn't you find him at the funeral?"

"Of course I did. He's on his way to the office. I'm talking about my father." Nicole sounded as though she wanted to add "you stupid old woman." "Are the police there?"

"Mr. Hammond is with an officer now," Betty said. "He is not taking calls."

"Tell him to call me as soon as he's free. And don't you dare tell anyone that I was there. I don't have time to waste talking to the police."

"I've already had to state who was here this morning," Betty said, "but I indicated that you were barely out of my sight."

"Keep it that way, or my father will have you fired."

Betty thought that might be a blessing but merely said, "I don't really work here, so don't trouble yourself. If you'd like to speak to your husband, they're just arriving from the funeral."

A forlorn and confused group of Zig-Zag employees, led by Jerry Preston, trailed in under the watchful eye of a young uniformed policeman.

"Have my father call me when he can," Nicole Preston said. "I've got to go out." She hung up.

Eileen looked frightened, Tanya defiant. The third young woman whom Betty took to be Marsha seemed on the brink of tears. Marsha was about thirty and bordered on plump. Her hair was an inexpertly contrived strawberry-blond. Mr. Caruso looked serious, Reuben the office boy looked uncomfortable. She noted that he wore an earring. Edwards & Son would never have permitted that in the old days. The two programmers were ill at ease in their jackets and ties and clearly wished they were elsewhere. At least most of the emergency people had departed, leaving only some crime-scene men still working in Denise's office.

"Betty, what's happening?" Eileen said tearfully. "They said another person is dead."

"Is it Amanda?" Tanya asked. "She wasn't at the funeral."

"I'm afraid so," Betty said. "I found her."

"How *awful*!" Eileen was half enjoying the sensation.

"Mr. Preston . . ." Marsha had a whining voice that Betty thought would irritate her thoroughly after a very brief time.

Betty said, "Mr. Preston, as soon as you're able, I need to speak to you privately. About some calls . . ."

"Is it okay?" Jerry asked their guard. The policeman shrugged his assent, and Betty took Jerry away to the visitors' chairs.

"I found her in Denise's office," Betty said softly. "Mr. Mitsui was here this morning." She hesitated and was about to tell him that Mr. Mitsui had actually found the body, in spite of his telephone call.

"Oh, no . . ." Jerry interrupted her, and sounded in total despair. "First Denise, then Amanda, and now Mitsui shows up in the middle of a godawful mess." He looked worried. "The Japanese are so touchy. Nicole will kill me if this screws up everything. George is already on a tear."

"Mr. Hammond arrived just before you did," Betty said. He might as well have all the bad news at once. "He's talking to the police. Someone called him."

In her own mind Betty was certain that his daughter Nicole had called him, not some person at the town hall. Nicole had seen Amanda dead in those few seconds she was in Jerry's office and she had wanted her father on the scene.

"This is terrible," Jerry said, and he managed to look terrible himself. "The constable didn't explain much when he caught up with me after the funeral."

"Mr. Preston." Marsha whined again, loudly. "Do I have to stay? I don't feel so good."

"The police will want to talk to all of us," Jerry said. "It's just routine. You'll have to hang on." The programmers shuffled, Reuben fingered his incipient mustache, and Mr. Caruso sighed heavily and took a seat. "A death like this is a serious thing."

"Don't forget Denise," Tanya said. She looked very elegant today in sober black but with a stunning African pendant on her breast and huge gold hoop earrings. "It was real serious for her, too."

"There's no reason to connect the two deaths," Jerry said sternly. Tanya didn't look convinced. Nobody did. "They have to eliminate possible suspects," he said. "I guess that's everybody except Betty here."

"I don't know 'bout that," Tanya said. She looked at Betty. "She was here for less than a day before she got into a fight with Amanda. I heard them. And she was here alone today."

"Really . . ." Betty began, but the trooper and George Hammond appeared.

"Jerry," Hammond said, "if this causes any trouble for my little girl, you're going to answer for it."

"George, I don't know anything about this."

"I'll see you tonight at your house," Hammond said, and marched out of Zig-Zag.

"You, Preston," the state trooper said. "One of the detectives wants to speak with you now." He pointed to Tanya. "And you come with me for a chat."

Tanya raised her chin defiantly and followed him toward the conference room. Her look back at Betty was not very friendly.

And I thought she liked my work, Betty thought ruefully.

"I got to go to the ladies' room," Marsha said. She put her hand instinctively to her right eye, and Betty thought she detected a bruise covered with makeup. She hurried away.

Eileen sat at her desk and looked downcast.

"This is *so* awful," she said. "And the funeral was real sad."

"Was there a man in a wheelchair at the service?" Betty asked.

"Yeah. He came in late." She wrinkled her little nose. "Ugh. I couldn't live like that. Marsha knows him. She lives over in East Moulton, you know? I mean, her husband, Mikie, works for him sometimes doing yardwork. You know him?"

"He's a neighbor," Betty said. Despite her irritating voice, Marsha suddenly seemed appealing: an unexpected source of information.

CHAPTER 11

"MISS TRENKA," the trooper said. "Miss Trenka, I am very, very disappointed in you."

They were seated alone at the conference table where earlier he had spoken to Tanya, Eileen, and finally Marsha. Betty waited to hear what had disappointed the trooper. Eileen might well have said that Betty had asked too many questions about Zig-Zag, and Tanya surely had mentioned Amanda's outburst yesterday as Betty had left Jerry's office, although probably everyone in the office had had a run-in with Amanda.

Did that make her a suspect? She decided to take the rational approach, the disinterested person above the fray.

"I suppose the girls are quite shaken," she said. "A lot of stress builds up quickly in a group when one person dies suddenly the way Miss Legrand did and now Miss Glyn. I used to be responsible for an office much larger than this one, but in my present position I have no control over the Zig-Zag staff."

"I'm not talking about your responsibility in keeping their emotions in check," he said. He looked at a paper among several he had in front of him on the table. "I'm referring to this Mr. Mitsui."

"Ah. Yes."

"He telephoned us." The trooper looked at her sternly. "He stated that he had been at Zig-Zag this morning, as you mentioned. However, he also confessed that when he passed an open office door, he saw the young woman lying on the floor, obviously dead. Being a foreigner faced with an apparent crime, he panicked."

Not likely, Betty thought, but attempted to look surprised and concerned. Apparently Mr. Mitsui had gotten through to Tokyo and received his instructions: innocent bystander.

"He said he then left abruptly, without informing you."

"Indeed."

"He felt it was his duty after all to explain to the authorities that he had nothing to do with the murder."

"How . . . how honorable. But why are you disappointed in me?"

"You knew he found the body," the trooper said. "That's what I think. And you neglected to mention the fact."

"You may think that," Betty said, "but I hesitate to contradict Mr. Mitsui."

"According to Hammond and Preston, he's an important guy, so for the moment we'll take his word. He claims he has no intention of fleeing our jurisdiction because he has continuing business here with Preston and George Hammond. Know anything about it?"

"Nothing."

"He knew this Denise Legrand professionally, but he claims he was safely tucked away in New York at the Waldorf when she was killed. And he says he can't remember ever seeing the dead girl before."

"He very likely saw her if he'd been to these offices before," Betty said wryly, "but I doubt if he noticed her. She was only a typist." She wondered why he was telling her these things.

"I can only assume that you were safely tucked away somewhere, too," he said, "like your good friend Mr. Mitsui."

"Me? Preposterous. And he's not a friend. I repeat, I only met Amanda on Monday. I never met Denise Legrand. What about all these other people who did know both of them?"

"We look into all possibilities," he said.

"So you are looking into whether Denise was killed on purpose. I knew it."

The trooper gazed at her. "Miss Trenka, if you know anything, I'd advise you to speak up."

"Oh, I don't 'know' anything," Betty said. "It simply occurred to me that even if you did intentionally run into a person with your car, you couldn't be sure the person was dead. I mean, if you wanted someone dead, you made sure."

"That will be all for now," the trooper said.

Betty continued as though he hadn't spoken. "You'd have to run over the body several times, I should think. Or use some weapon." She looked at him expectantly. "I suppose you don't want to tell me what happened."

The trooper gave in. "It's going to come out as soon as we start talking to a lot of people. The papers have gotten ahold of the real story. Miss Legrand wasn't run over. She was struck in the head and killed."

"Ah! The proverbial blunt instrument. What sort?"

"That's all," he said firmly. "Just be sure to let us know if anything else 'occurs' to you."

She decided not to mention her own telephone call from Mr. Mitsui.

Since Jerry Preston had either departed for a late lunch or was still in conference with the police, Betty made her way to the accounting office, past an uncommunicative Eileen, who kept her eyes on her *Bride's* magazine. The atmosphere at Zig-Zag was distinctly gloomy, although the fluorescent lighting continued to glow brightly and a pale sun was a faint disk behind a thin layer of clouds.

Two definite murders. Both of them the result of being struck on the head. Two women who worked for the same company. Betty shivered at the thought. Was anyone else in danger?

Reuben was visible at the end of the corridor standing in the copier room apparently doing nothing.

Betty remembered the key she had sworn to return and hailed him. Reuben looked up, startled.

"I have the key," she said as she approached him. "The key to the door so I could get in today."

He put out his hand.

"I mean, it's in my handbag, in the accounting room. I'll just get it." She stopped. "Are there many keys distributed among the employees?"

"Some," he said. Reuben had not spoken enough for her to determine whether he had an accent, but he certainly did appear to be vaguely Hispanic. She wondered whether many Latins had found their way to the neighborhood of East Moulton and Hammond Center. Assimilation in old New England towns had never been easy. She knew that from experience.

"About how many?" Betty persisted, even though Reuben was beginning to look somewhat alarmed.

"I told the police already," he said. "What you want to know for?"

Betty stood up straight and put on her kind but determined look, a woman not willing to brook any nonsense and not one who needed to explain her reasons for asking. It seemed to work.

"The boss," Reuben said, just this side of sullen defiance. "Miss Legrand. Two of the girls share the other— Marsha and Tanya. I got one, the one you have."

"Not Amanda?"

"She don't need a key. She got friends."

"Friends? What do you mean?"

"Nothing. I don't mean nothing," he said.

"It's quite odd-looking, the key you gave me. I suppose it's hard to duplicate."

"Only one place to get one like that," Reuben said. "You have to get Mr. Preston's written permission. Or Mr. Hammond's."

He was eyeing her with considerable suspicion now, but she forged ahead. "How do the programmers get in then? I understand they work all hours, day and night."

"Separate door out back. The door into programming is always locked, both sides. They don't like the girls around bothering them. I go down there sometimes when I got work. You with the cops or something?"

"No, just nosy," Betty said. "Let me get your key."

Tanya was busy at her computer terminal and did not look around when Betty came in. Marsha had not gone home but sat at her terminal, the one Betty had used the day before. Her fingers rested on the keyboard, but she was staring at a blank screen.

"I didn't introduce myself . . ." Betty said. Marsha gasped and jumped. "Sorry. I'm Betty Trenka. We spoke yesterday. I was hoping to run out for a sandwich since I don't have much to do at the moment. Do you think you could join me?"

"Get her outta here," Tanya said, without taking her eyes from her screen. "I can't work with her sniffling around like she lost her best friend."

"You sure it's okay?" Marsha looked anxiously at Tanya's back. "Usually I bring lunch, it saves money, but I didn't have time this morning, getting the kids off to school and Mike to work, and then I had to get ready for the funeral." Marsha was speaking very fast, as if on some sort of automatic pilot.

"Ain't nothing going on here, and you sure aren't getting any high marks for exceptional effort today."

"What about your lunch?" Marsha was still anxious, but at least she wasn't whining now.

"Who could eat with all these dead bodies around?" Tanya waved them away. Her big gold earrings jiggled as she shook her head and bent to her work.

Betty put on her coat and opened her handbag. "I'll just return this key to Reuben." She looked up. Marsha was staring at the key in her hand with something like terror. "What is it, Marsha?"

"Nothing," Marsha said quickly. "Nothing at all. I just remembered that I . . . I forgot my key. It's my week to have it." She tried a smile. Actually she was quite pretty.

"Where will we go?" Betty said brightly to divert Marsha from the apparently terrifying key.

"I know this place we go sometimes. It's down in Hammond Center."

Betty pictured one of the fast-food places in the minimall complete with fries heaped in a cardboard container, a burger on a paper plate, and a handful of plastic cutlery. Not much of a step up from prepackaged microwaved meals.

The corridor was empty. Reuben wasn't in the copier room. Eileen told them that Jerry had sent him out to buy lunch. Betty put the key away in her bag.

"I'd like to drive myself, if you don't mind," she said. "I want to get to know the area better." She also wanted to gauge how long a walk Amanda might have had to come from Hammond Center to Zig-Zag. "I just moved from upstate to East Moulton. I understand you live there, too."

Marsha shrugged. "I've lived there my whole life. Married a guy I went to high school with." She didn't sound entirely happy about that. "Two kids. My girl does real good in school, fifth grade. The boy has this learning disability, they say. They got him in special-ed classes."

"The people in town seem nice," Betty said.

"There's all kinds," Marsha said as they reached the cluster of stores that constituted the Hammond Center minimall. "Take a right here at the traffic light." She seemed in better spirits.

Betty thought Amanda could have managed the distance easily and wondered if her car was parked somewhere around the shops.

A short distance away from the little mall with its nearly identical plastic signs and rows of identical-looking shops was a street of old-fashioned wooden buildings. It was no doubt the original Hammond Center, passed by in the rush of progress. Marsha pointed to a parking space in front of a one-story building set close to the street: Mom's Luncheonette.

Inside, the room was full of mismatched chairs and tables, but there were bright tablecloths and cloth napkins, with little vases of fall flowers at the center of each table.

Only a few people were still finishing lunch. Betty hoped that "Mom" got more business earlier in the lunch hour.

Marsha ordered a salad—she claimed to be dieting, but she nervously consumed several rolls with butter before lunch arrived. Betty had the split pea with ham soup of the day.

"Tell me about Denise and Amanda," Betty said, businesslike. She had decided that this was the best approach for Marsha. Sentiment and sorrow would only get her weepy again.

It appeared, however, to have been a poor choice. Marsha's large blue eyes welled up with impending tears.

"It's all my fault that Mandy's dead," she said, and gulped back a sob. The tears spilled over and made a path through the makeup covering the bruise on her cheek.

"You certainly didn't kill her," Betty said firmly, although for all she knew Marsha had indeed wielded the deadly ceramic pot.

Firmness worked this time.

"I could never kill *anything*, even something awful like a mouse!" The tears stopped. "It's just that Amanda had my key to the building. Tanya and I have it every other week, you know? So in case Denise or Reuben are late or something, the rest of us can get in. This was my week to have it. Amanda called me at home yesterday and then drove over to my house after work to borrow it. She said she wanted to get into the office early this morning, now that Denise was dead. If I hadn't given it to her, she'd be alive now." She blinked. The tears were close to reappearing. "It must have been a robber."

"Have there been robberies at Zig-Zag?"

"Well . . . no. Not really. There's not much to steal, is there? Software programs, but you can buy them at computer stores. Nothing special."

Marsha seemed unaware of the new software release Jerry had talked about, so Betty decided not to mention it. She also avoided mentioning the logical next step: If it wasn't a robber, then it must have been someone whom

Amanda and perhaps the others at Zig-Zag knew. "So Amanda wanted to use your key to get in very early. To do some of Denise's work?"

Marsha shrugged. "She didn't really have work besides what Jerry or Mr. Caruso had her do. Of course, when Mr. Hammond was in the office, she was real eager to help him. She told me that's how you got to the top, the way Denise did. She helped Tanya and me, but she hated doing the receivables. She thought she was too important for that." She hesitated. "She used to try to come on to Jerry, you know? Even Mr. Hammond." Marsha whispered now, although there was no one else to hear. "I told her it was no good getting mixed up with the boss. I think she went out to dinner with Jerry, and even once with Mr. Hammond. She said Jerry's wife didn't care, but I didn't believe *that*."

"Did you ever mention Amanda's little escapades around the office?"

"No, but Denise probably knew. Anyhow, Amanda couldn't keep a secret. Eileen never came out and said it, but Amanda probably told her. She was, like, competing for Jerry with Denise. And she was . . . well, nosy. Maybe she wanted the key to get in to look at things she wasn't supposed to know about."

"Such as?"

Marsha looked uncomfortable. "I wasn't, like, real friendly with Denise. She was so . . ." She searched for the right descriptive words. "Sophisticated, older. You know. But she got along better with me than with the others. We talked some, you know? She said big things were coming and not to say anything. Well, I didn't because I didn't know what she was talking about. She and Jerry pretty much ran everything, except for Mrs. Preston around giving advice. And Mr. Hammond."

Betty said gently, "You did say something to me yesterday about Denise being killed on purpose."

"Yeah, but I didn't really think . . . The first person I thought of was Amanda. She wanted to be Denise, to have her job and all, but now there's Amanda dead. It's scary. Denise said . . ." Marsha fiddled with the end of a roll. She balled up her napkin and then flattened it out. "She said something last week. She was joking, in a real good mood. She said, 'If I get out of this week alive, it'll be miracle. Otherwise, *sayonara*.' Then she laughed."

"What? *Sayonara?*"

"It's Japanese. It means good-bye, but it wasn't like she was serious. Now, look what's happened. You don't think . . . That Mr. Mitsui is awful quiet and polite."

"Don't be silly," Betty said. "He's just a businessman. Denise was probably speaking figuratively about business."

Marsha looked half convinced. "Mike, that's my husband, is always after me to quit working, but we need the money and I like having a job. The kids don't suffer; I take care of Mike okay." She looked down at the remains of her salad. "Now he'll say two murders and maybe I'll be next if I don't get out of there. When Mike gets mad . . ." She stopped.

"So you can't think of any reason Amanda would be at the office, except to snoop," Betty said hastily. She wasn't prepared at this time to hear about Marsha's domestic troubles.

"Well . . ." Marsha pondered the question for a time. "Maybe she was meeting someone?"

That was rather what Betty thought. "Reuben said the strangest thing. Amanda didn't need a key because she had friends. I suppose he meant you and Tanya could lend the key."

"Maybe," Marsha said slowly. "I just feel sick about this every time I think of the two of them. . . ."

Before Marsha could think any more, Betty pushed on. "Tell me about East Moulton. I've met a few people in town. A Mrs. Brown and Edward Kelso. Do you know them?"

Marsha cheered up a bit. "Mike works for Mr. Kelso on weekends. He has this big garden out back, and bees."

"Bees? Honey bees?"

"His hobby, since he can't do a lot of stuff because of the wheelchair. Mrs. Brown—boy, do I know about her. Everybody in town does. She likes to run things at the church and when there are town events. She's supposed to be rich, but maybe she just acts that way. Her son Alan's a lot older than me, but I sure had a crush on him when I was in high school. He was *so* handsome. Denise . . ." She stopped again. "I didn't really understand, but years ago there was something between Denise and Alan. My mom says that Mrs. Brown put a stop to it because Denise was, like, ten years older. Denise went away, and Alan still lives with his mother in that big house on Prospect Street. It's almost next door to Denise's place. I'll bet Mrs. Brown hated it when Denise moved there after she came back to town. Wow, look at the time. Tanya will be wild if I take too long."

Betty paid the modest check for both of them. When she reached the street, Marsha was standing at the curb gazing thoughtfully at a long black limousine parked at the end of the block.

"Look at that," Marsha said. "There's nothing around here anybody in a car like that would want."

Betty frowned, then hurried Marsha toward her car.

Although she couldn't be certain, it looked remarkably like the limo that had brought Mr. Mitsui to Zig-Zag.

As she headed back, Betty kept her eye on the rearview mirror, but Mr. Mitsui had apparently decided not to pursue her to the gates of Zig-Zag.

Jerry Preston looked harried when he asked Betty to come to the office he'd taken over until the police were finished in his.

"Tell me again what Mitsui said when he was here."

"He didn't say a thing," Betty said. "He asked for you and Denise and then Mr. Hammond. He waited around in the conference room and made some calls, then he left."

"Before the police came."

"Yes."

"I can't locate him, and he hasn't called. I don't know what all Denise might have promised him on my behalf.

She'd laid out our strategy. Now I'm under suspicion in two murders. *Two.* I had no reason to kill either of them, but I have no way of proving where I was. I went out, and when I got home, my wife was asleep. I told them I slept in the den so I wouldn't wake her. My wife is furious. My father-in-law is in a rage. The girls here are hysterical. What am I going to do?"

As long as he asked, Betty offered a temporary solution. "Close the offices early. Send everybody home. Go home yourself. Go jogging. Take a hot bath."

"What if Mitsui calls?"

"You do have something he wants?"

Jerry nodded. "I do. I think he wants it badly."

"Then he'll call again."

Jerry's smile was bleak. "You're right. Absolutely. Tell the girls to go home, will you? Thanks."

Betty Trenka, for however briefly, was in charge again.

CHAPTER 12

As BETTY drove away from Zig-Zag, her thoughts returned to her lunchtime conversation with Marsha: the question of the key, Amanda's alleged flirtations. She wondered if it was the case of the younger woman trying to show up the older Denise and, indeed, perhaps emulate her.

Too bad, Betty thought, that she had never seen Denise. She must have been an exotic bloom in this peaceful neighborhood. No one had said she was beautiful, but she must have had both style and a strong personality to have evoked so many different responses.

It was late enough in the afternoon that Eve should already be home from school, so Betty turned on Main Street in East Moulton to drive to the white farmhouse and the produce stand at the bottom on the Prospect Street hill. Eve might be terrified by the thought of talking to the police, but she might be willing to answer Betty's gentler questions about the night Denise was killed and what she had seen.

The produce stand was bare today, and the curtains in the front room of the house were drawn. A very large black-and-white cat examined her with hostile yellow eyes from its perch on the veranda railing. No one was visible near the big red barn, nor was anyone to be seen out in the fields where the rows of cornstalks were beginning to turn brown and dry. A field of cabbages and squash was still thriving and green, and tomato plants along the side of the house were heavy with late red and green tomatoes. There were no vehicles parked in the rutted drive between the house and the barn except for a derelict piece of farm machinery with grass growing high around its wheels.

Betty saw no doorbell, so she knocked loudly on the front door.

The woman who opened it after a short wait looked haggard and careworn, although she was barely middle-aged. Her hands were rough, but she was still slim and had probably once been as pretty as Eve.

"Have you heard something?" she asked eagerly before Betty could speak.

"No," Betty said, surprised. "Mrs. . . ." She realized she didn't know the family name. "My name is Elizabeth Trenka. I met your daughter Eve . . . Evelyn on Sunday." She gestured toward the stand.

Eve's mother didn't seem to hear her. The hope that had briefly lighted up her face was gone.

"I wanted to speak to her if she's home," Betty said.

"She's gone," the woman said dully. "Yesterday or last night. She didn't come home. Her father's been out looking for her all day all over town."

Betty didn't think Evelyn-Evangeline-Eve would be found in East Moulton. She imagined her in a car with that long-haired boy heading west toward the setting sun and the Pacific Ocean.

"Are you one of her teachers?" Eve's mother asked. She seemed not to have heard Betty at all.

"No. I happened to meet her on Sunday. I just moved to town."

"She's gone," the woman said. "If she left with that boy, her father will kill them both. And her brothers will, too. She's our youngest. The only girl. Her father's little girl."

"I'm so sorry," Betty said, not knowing what else to say. "Have you notified the police?"

The woman looked alarmed. "Joe don't hold with the police. She's run off like she kept saying she would. I blame these fancy women who come here in their big cars and put ideas in Evie's head. I blame the Legrand woman. All that makeup and traveling I don't know where."

"Perhaps Evelyn was upset about her death," Betty said.

"She got what she deserved, all that carrying on. Why, she was older than me. I knew her when I was a kid."

"Carrying on?"

"Everybody knows. Poor Alan Brown and then that crippled man. I've heard all the stories. She wasn't good for my little girl. I say Denise Legrand got what was coming to her."

Oh, dear, Betty thought. Someone else who didn't care for Denise. This wasn't going anywhere, and it was time to ease away. If Eve had actually seen something of the "accident" that had ended Denise's life, this would be the time to flee from her discontent at home, taking her knowledge with her.

What had Eve said? She'd figured out a way to get away.

Betty wasn't sure how she should go about sharing her suspicions with the authorities, or even if she should say anything at all. She hated to do it: bring Eve back to face the certain wrath of her father and the questions of the police.

"If Eve comes home," Betty said, "please have her call me. My number . . ." She couldn't think of her new number. "It's a new number. The information operator will have it. Timberhill Road."

"You're the one who bought Molly's uncle's place. They were talking about you in the drugstore."

Betty shuddered inwardly. "Were they, indeed? Who?"

"Just people." Eve's mother started to close the door. "They were saying the police were at your house last night." She looked at Betty guardedly.

"They were asking about a neighbor," Betty said. She didn't think Ted Kelso would welcome being referred to as the "crippled man," even in his absence. She supposed that Penny Saks or one of her boys had seen the trooper at her door.

"They said it was about Denise Legrand. They think he

ran her down. The woman's causing trouble even from her grave. You know what she was like."

"I never met her," Betty said. "Thank you for your time."

She sat in her car for a moment. Gossip was a small town's favorite entertainment, but she was mildly annoyed that she had so quickly become a topic of conversation. Of course people would speculate about a new resident, but this was too much. Then she sighed, resigned to being the wonder of the week. It would all be forgotten soon. Ted Kelso's reputation wasn't faring well either at the moment, if the gossips were casting him as a murderer.

Betty headed home, driving slowly across the bridge where Denise had died and up Prospect Street. She saw a big white house with green trim and a stone walk leading up from the road. It fit the description Eve had given of Denise's house. It looked desolate for some reason, although Denise had only been dead a few days. Then she realized that all the shades were down so the house looked blindly out through the trees to the street. Farther up the street she passed a large, rather old-fashioned house set way back from the road, and she thought she glimpsed a handsome golden retriever in a stately pose in back among the birches and firs. She imagined it was Alan Brown's running companion, and that it was here that Alan and his mother lived in sight of Denise's house.

She had three hours before she would report on her day to Ted Kelso. There were still unopened cartons in the spare bedroom, and boxes of kitchen items she hadn't put away. But they—and the projected new curtains for the living room—held no interest for her today.

Her report to Ted would be an unexpectedly long one: another murder; a visit from a Japanese businessman who had discovered the body but who had escaped police questions for the moment; a young company president who couldn't quite prove his whereabouts for either death; his arrogant and probably unhappy wife and his blustering father-in-law, who—Betty suddenly recalled Sid Senior's long-ago warning—wrote the checks, at least figuratively, for money that was his to start with; the state trooper who had stated that Denise had been struck on the head and not hit by a car at all; her co-worker who had heard Denise joke about getting out of the week alive—with Japanese overtones; and finally a missing girl who had likely seen something related to Denise's death.

An awful thought came to mind: She and Eve's mother had assumed that Eve had run away. What if Denise's murderer knew that Eve had seen something, had silenced her, and now she, too, was dead, somewhere in the woods off Prospect Street?

Betty shook her head. It couldn't be. Eve had taken off into the unknown to escape her fear and find her golden dreams. The only person who suspected she knew something was Betty.

As she turned into her driveway, Penny Saks came loping across the field, waving to her. She was wearing jeans and a sweatshirt and looked scarcely older than Eve.

"Betty . . . it's okay to call you Betty, isn't it? I was worried. There's someone in your house."

"What? Who?"

"A man. He went to your door and he went right in."

"Goodness. Did I forget to lock the door?" She knew she was sometimes forgetful nowadays and hoped it wasn't an insidious sign of advancing age. "Is it someone you know from around town?"

"No," Penny said, "but I think he must be okay. He came in a limousine."

Betty closed her eyes. She didn't really want to see Mr. Mitsui just now.

"It's all right, Penny," Betty said airily. "I know who he is. He's definitely okay." Then Denise's *"sayonara"* came to mind, and she didn't feel quite so confident.

"That's a relief," Penny said. "I don't think I've ever seen a car like that in East Moulton."

Betty thought she detected a tiny note of respectful awe.

"It's only business," she said. "Some executives have healthy expense accounts."

"If you can stand the boys," Penny said, "come to dinner next week, okay? We'll pick a night when Greg isn't out talking to prospects."

"That would be nice, thank you." If Mr. Mitsui had taken the liberty of entering her house, she thought he deserved to wait while she chatted with her neighbor. "I'm having dinner tonight with Ted Kelso. So kind of him to invite me. Somebody said he keeps bees."

"Yes, isn't that cute? The boys are crazy about them. Whitey is fearless, but they scare me." She looked at Betty as though she had something more to say but didn't know how to say it. "I saw the police here last night. Any problem?"

So it had probably been Penny who had carelessly spread the word at the drugstore.

"They wanted to see Ted Kelso, but he wasn't at home, so they came to my house. That's all."

"I told Greg it was nothing." She made it sound as though Greg had expressed grave doubts about the new neighbor.

"Here's some news that you're sure to hear around town." Betty decided to give Penny something to really think about. "A young woman was found dead this morning at Zig-Zag, the company where I'm working."

"No! Who was it? Isn't that where Denise Legrand worked?" Penny looked halfway between thrilled and shocked. "Two of them from the same company. How awful! How did it happen?"

"It was a typist named Amanda Glyn who was in the office very early. It appears that she was murdered. Since I found her body, you may see the police here again. Now, I ought to see what my visitor wants. It's business," she repeated, to forestall further gossip about gentleman callers in limousines.

"I'll let you know about dinner," Penny said. "Wait till Greg hears about the murder." She was off again across the field, dying for the return of her husband to tell her tale to, or more likely to get on the phone to be the first to give her friends the news of this latest sensation.

Betty opened her front door. The living room was dim, but she saw Mr. Mitsui sitting in one of the dark blue armchairs she'd brought from the old apartment. He looked peaceful, with his hands folded across his chest and his hat resting on his knees.

"What a surprise to see you again so soon, Mr. Mitsui. Shall I put water on for tea? Or perhaps you'd care for a sherry?"

He stood up, hat in hand, and bowed very slightly. "I do not intend to stay long," he said. "A matter of a few minutes."

Betty waited while he arranged his thoughts.

"I wish to thank you again for being . . . so careful about my visit to your offices this morning. It saved me great trouble."

Betty dismissed his thanks with a wave of her hand. "I did what I felt was right under the circumstances. One has an obligation to the company one works for."

"Company loyalty is most important," Mr. Mitsui said. "I find the younger workers in my country are becoming less devoted to the idea. Have the authorities learned who committed the crime?"

"Two crimes, I afraid, Mr. Mitsui. Not only did someone kill Miss Glyn, but Denise Legrand was deliberately murdered."

He frowned. "This is terrible." He looked genuinely troubled by the news. "You are certain she was murdered?"

"As sure as I can be," Betty said. "The information comes from the police."

"Ah. This changes my plans," he said. He started toward the door.

"Mr. Mitsui," she said sternly, "you entered my home uninvited."

"The door was unlocked," he said almost humbly.

"At least you owe me some explanation for your visit.

Perhaps you would care to tell me whether the two deaths are somehow connected with your dealings with Zig-Zag and Mr. Preston."

He looked at her with some respect. "You are quite intelligent," he said. Perhaps in his mind he finished the sentence with "for a woman," but Betty didn't care. She wanted to know.

"The connection?" she asked again.

"That would be difficult to determine," Mr. Mitsui said. He gazed at her, weighing his words. Finally he said, "I know very little of the young woman I found dead this morning. I have seen her on earlier visits, she is very . . . mmm." Words failed him in describing Amanda. "She was a child, not important in the company. Miss Legrand was quite important." He hesitated. "She was acting as our agent in negotiating for certain products produced or soon to be produced by Zig-Zag. Now I find that her death was not an accident, so I must review my plans. My organization will wish to be most careful about . . . difficulties that could arise from these murders."

"She was a secret agent for your organization?" Betty fastened on his startling revelation.

"Not at all," he said soothingly. "She represented our interests since I could not always be at hand. Of course, she did not make this known to Mr. Preston or Mr. Hammond."

"How did you find her to act for you—to represent your interests, as you put it?"

"That would be difficult to say," Mr. Mitsui said.

Betty had had enough nonsense today. "Nevertheless, please try." She made it a point to draw herself up to her full height and look down on him.

"I did not find her," he said. "She found us."

"Please explain."

"It is not possible to do so at this time." His statement had a definite finality to it.

"I see," Betty said, but did not. "Why are you here?"

"I came with the intention of suggesting that you replace

her in the same role, but I will not do so now because of the murders."

"I am glad that you did not ask me," Betty said severely. "I would have refused." He seemed not to know that she was only a temporary employee at Zig-Zag with no standing whatsoever.

"I saw that you are in a position of trust," he began.

"Not at all," she said.

"But this must be so, as Mr. Hammond would not entrust a woman with the work of his company if she was without wisdom."

So George Hammond was the puppeteer as well as the man with the money, while poor Jerry yearned to be with his computers but was instead stuck in the executive suite, perhaps merely a figurehead.

"Why would you think I would become your . . . agent?" She was moderately flattered by his presumption of her status and spoke with authority, not at all like a temporary typist whose career at Zig-Zag was to end on Wednesday. If Mr. Mitsui brought up her name with George Hammond or Jerry, he would no doubt lose considerable face when he was told who she really was. Well, that was his problem.

"The money is very good," he said simply. "Miss Legrand was most interested in our future plans for her. You, too, would have benefited greatly. My organization may still wish to offer—"

"I will hear no more of this," Betty said severely, "and I trust you will inform the police of Miss Legrand's actual and projected roles."

Mr. Mitsui met her eyes, but said nothing.

"Otherwise," Betty said, "I may feel obliged to inform them myself."

He almost smiled. "There is no proof of her role. It was an understanding that died with her. I do not think the police will readily believe you, since you have already told them a slight untruth about me. I could confirm this to them."

He had her there.

"I think our meeting is over," she said.

"I believe we will meet again, Miss Trenka," he said, and bowed again, this time a bit more deeply. He took a very small cellular phone from his pocket and dialed. "I am ready," she heard him say.

By the time he had walked through the door and down the path to the roadside, the limousine had pulled up. The driver came around to open the door for him and in another moment Mr. Mitsui was driven away.

Betty watched him go. So his secret arrangement had died with Denise. What had died with Amanda? Some other secret, surely. Could she have known something about Denise's role and been silenced? If so, who would benefit from the two deaths?

The answer that immediately came to mind was Mr. Mitsui. His plans might be askew, but if Denise had made demands . . . She shook her head. If Denise had been discovered as a spy in the corporate bosom . . . Betty needed to talk about this with someone she trusted to set everything straight in her mind. In the old days she would have taken it to Sid Senior. They would have talked as friends and colleagues, but those days were over. She would soon be talking to Ted Kelso, but she did not entirely trust him.

She was on her own.

CHAPTER 13

She was almost on her own. She could share some things with Ted Kelso, even though he was not an intimate or even a friend yet. All they had was a sort of business relationship pertaining to Denise and Zig-Zag, and she didn't know his real role in all of this.

This dinner was simply a matter of business. Still, she was looking forward to the coming evening with her interesting if somewhat intimidating neighbor.

As the hour of her appointment approached, Betty thought it didn't feel right going empty-handed to dinner at her new neighbor's, but Ted Kelso had sounded so firm about it. She never went to Cora and Dave Welles's place without a bottle of wine or a simple dessert. She supposed the habit grew out of her childhood in a small Connecticut factory town where her parents never went to eat at the home of friends without carrying a plate of poppyseed buns or warm plum-stuffed dumplings dusted with sugar.

Out back there were still a few late roses on the over-grown rosebushes, but if the man kept bees, he certainly had plenty of flowers already. She had no wine in the house, but she wouldn't have known what to bring even if she'd thought of it in time. She had nothing. Perhaps it was just as well.

The clouds had blown away in the afternoon and now the sky was pale blue as the sun began to sink. Betty turned on the news and watched it for a while. The world was not a better place today than it had been yesterday. There was no story about Amanda's death, but it must have seemed an insignificant event to the Hartford, New Haven, and Providence channels. The *Ledger* tossed on her doorstep also had no story.

While she was changing into a nice dark green silk blouse and a beige linen skirt, Betty reflected on her situation. She was caught up briefly in a complicated series of events that really didn't have much to do with her. She regretted the two deaths, but she didn't think she'd ever know the full story. At best, she'd hear who'd done it. The official story wouldn't satisfy anyone, and the rest would be opinion and speculation. Yet she had to admit that she did want to know *why* as well as *who*.

Eve's disappearance worried her. The more she thought about it, the more it seemed that Eve must have been frightened and confused by what Betty imagined she'd seen. Eve was not quite the daughter—granddaughter, rather—that Betty didn't have, but she represented all of the unformed, inexperienced young women who had come to work under Betty over the years and who had managed to learn from her some principles of business and hard work. Some had resented it, but several had taken the time, years later, to get in touch with her to thank her for the training. A few had managed to convey, along with their thanks, a mild disdain for Betty's own failure to rise higher in the company, to seize the opportunities; they had done "much better."

Betty would gently remind them that times were different for them. Young women of her day had different expectations, indeed lived in a different world. She had done all right nevertheless. If only they knew.

She looked at herself in the mirror as she brushed on a bit of blusher on each cheek. Well enough, she supposed, but getting booted out of Edwards & Son still rankled.

She wouldn't let Ted Kelso see through to her feelings about that again. He was a sharp observer, although she'd never heard that confinement to a wheelchair made a person more aware of others' feelings. It certainly hadn't mellowed him, whatever the cause of his disability. He might tell her about himself one day, unless it turned out he was involved in these deaths.

No, she decided, he simply could not be a factor in Denise's death; definitely not in Amanda's. She thought she wouldn't mention Mr. Mitsui's alleged relationship with Denise or the fact that Denise had apparently been instrumental in putting Mr. Mitsui together with Zig-Zag by likely telling him about Jerry's top-secret program. She would definitely not mention that she had told a half-truth on Mr. Mitsui's behalf. She was sorry now that she'd done it. And she absolutely would not speak of Mr. Mitsui's intended proposal to her.

At exactly seven o'clock Betty crossed Timberhill Road and rang Ted Kelso's bell. It was still fairly light, but the porch light was on and no voice spoke through the intercom. Ted opened the door within seconds of her ring.

"Right on time. I didn't expect anything less," he said. "And not a sour-cream dip in sight. Good woman. Come along. If my information is correct, you've got a lot to tell me."

Betty blinked at his voice of command but followed as he smoothly moved ahead of her toward the kitchen and dining area. The smell of good food was a happy relief after all her recent boring dinners.

The table was set with red placemats, large black plates, black cloth napkins with red stitching on the borders, and three velvety red roses in a slim black vase.

"What a charming table," she said. The wine glasses looked to be of delicate crystal.

"I have plenty of time to think about details," Ted said. "Sit down. Have a drink? I got us a decent Chardonnay."

"That would be nice," Betty said. She supposed that was the correct response. She could always confess that Chardonnays had never been her strong suit if pressed to comment on matters of bouquet and vintage.

"Then fetch the glasses from the table. It's too much trouble to wash extra crystal by hand." He opened the refrigerator and took out a bottle of wine. "This may be too modest for someone who has men in limousines calling in the afternoon."

"You saw that. It was only Mr. Mitsui. He thinks I am more important than I am."

He poured the pale white wine into the two glasses she held. "I doubt that Mr. Mitsui makes many mistakes. Get started with your report. I hope you like lobster, by the way. I forgot to ask if you were allergic or otherwise ill disposed toward creatures of the sea. No? Good. I drove down to the coast before dawn to get them, before I went to the funeral." He gestured toward a big pot on the boil on the ceramic cooktop.

"Really?" She sipped her wine. "Out so early?" Did she now have to be concerned about another person who had been out and about when Amanda was probably killed? "Did you know Amanda Glyn at all?" The wine was excellent.

"Only by reputation. A slinky young wench with few qualifications but high ambitions. Denise mentioned her, not kindly." Ted had a wry smile. "Rumor has it there was a brief office indiscretion, possibly involving Jerry Preston, but it isn't a proven thing by any means. Well?"

Betty decided to offer her most stunning news at once and get it over with. "The police told me that Denise had been struck on the head and killed and wasn't hit by a car at all. Now Amanda Glyn is dead, too. Clearly murdered. Hit on the head with a big glazed ceramic flowerpot in Denise's office."

"Ah, Denise's plants. I got her started with some special things. What else?"

"She was found—that is, I found her in Denise's office this morning. It evidently happened very early today."

"Another Zig-Zag murder. Imagine that." He sounded more sarcastic than surprised. "Go on."

"You knew?"

"The state policeman has become very attentive," Ted said. "I think his name is Roberts or Russell. He wanted to know my whereabouts early today and explained why.

They're not convinced I didn't have something to do with Denise's death, so they're trying to turn me into a homicidal maniac. I pointed out that a man in a wheelchair isn't much of a match for a healthy and mobile young woman like Amanda, whom I didn't know in any case. Then I suggested he call down to Addie's Fish Market on Route 1 near Saybrook about my dawn visit. You look relieved."

"I am. I wouldn't care to dine with a double murderer."

"Aha! You still suspect me, too, but you yourself said no car had hit her, and that's really my only weapon. So, Elizabeth, put that possibility out of your mind. We've got a lot to figure out. Tell me everything about today, exactly the way it happened."

This time his commanding tone was almost too much.

"As you already know about Amanda," she said coolly, "and I've told you about Denise, there's not much more to tell."

Ted Kelso gazed off over Betty's head. "It's so hard," he said. "I can't get around easily to ask the right questions. Here I am with my friend—I might even say, best friend—dead. The police still wonder if I might have been involved, however unlikely that is. I need your help." He looked down at his hands, and Betty felt momentarily guilty about making a hard life even harder.

"Yes, of course. I understand," she said. "I'm sorry. I'll try to help if I can."

"Good," he said, and then she saw him grinning at her.

"You *are* a master of manipulation, aren't you?" she said crossly.

"Always have been." Ted was cheerful in admitting it. "Why don't you just tell me everything and be as accurate as I'm sure you habitually are." He swung around and took a small case from a nearby shelf, flipped open the top, and rested the laptop computer on his lap. "I'm ready," he said.

Betty gave up and told him—up to her own predetermined point. It was a challenge to be exact. She wished she'd made notes along the way: Nicole Preston arriving in a rage; Mr. Mitsui's appearance at Zig-Zag; Amanda alive only yesterday and rather naked in her ambition to replace Denise, Amanda dead this morning; her call to the emergency services àfter finding Amanda; and the arrival of the police. The arrival of George Hammond.

"I'm not clear about the chain of command. Jerry's the president, but George Hammond seems to pull the strings."

"The Hammonds are used to being in charge. The family is quite well off, and they've lived around here for decades. Nicole's father bankrolled Zig-Zag and put it in one of the buildings he owns in that office park he dreamt up for the family land. Denise didn't indicate that he was deeply involved in Zig-Zag, but he dotes on Nicole and wants Jerry's business to be a success. He's a widower with a big place near Hammond Center, so he has plenty of time to help Nicole continue her life as a spoiled princess. Jerry's a smart guy, brilliant even when it comes to computers, but he's not cut out to be a prince consort. He belongs in an advanced computer lab at MIT."

"Denise didn't like Nicole. Of course, I got that from Amanda, who didn't like Denise, and whom apparently Nicole didn't like," Betty explained.

"Denise and Nicole met both socially and through the business, and there was no love lost. Denise had an old flame who was once a beau of Nicole's. The usual small-town stuff—he would have been the perfect mate for Nicole, but she met Jerry when she was at college near Boston. Denise thought her old boyfriend was her perfect mate, but she wasn't his social class and there was an unacceptable age gap. Everything's forgotten except the obligatory coolness that never goes away."

"How interesting," Betty said. He should know that Denise's old romance with Alan Brown hadn't been forgotten by the town's gossips with long memories. "The boyfriend would be Alan Brown. Would it have been Alan who recommended Denise for the job at Zig-Zag through his old friend Nicole Preston?"

"That has nothing to do with this," Ted said, and sounded angry. "Anyhow, Denise was focused on her future. The new product they're about to release. Denise gave me a copy, and I've been trying it out. It could be one of those things that becomes an international standard. I use Norton and some of those programs that handle computer viruses, but Jerry's is really amazing. It kills these computer viruses that plague us better than penicillin. It actually vaccinates software against both disease and hackers."

"That's what Mr. Preston meant," Betty said, half to herself. "The cure . . ."

"It's good work, worth a lot in the great computerized world out there. Go on."

"What?" She had been thinking of the implications of Denise realizing the potential value of the new software and bringing Mitsui in and acting as his agent. "Oh, about the office."

She told him about the sneakers Amanda had been wearing and her thought that either she'd walked to Zig-Zag before dawn or had been driven there by her murderer.

"Aha! Someone she knew."

"It occurred to me that she had arranged to meet someone." She told him about her lunch with Marsha, about Amanda borrowing the key and the curious thing Denise had said: "If I get out of this week alive . . ." and "sayonara."

"She didn't get out alive," Ted said. "Not a very subtle reference to your friend Mr. Mitsui."

"Oh, really! He was Denise's ally. She brought him into this Zig-Zag business." Betty realized immediately that she'd made a slip, and Ted had caught it.

"How do you know that?" He looked at her intently.

"I assumed." Betty decided on an outright lie.

Ted Kelso looked as though he did not believe her. He said, "Would you mind getting the lobsters from the refrigerator and dumping them into the pot? Does that trouble you?"

"I have no emotional ties to crustaceans," she said. "I used to do it all the time when we went to the beach when

I was a child." She dropped the two large lobsters into the boiling water.

Betty had a sudden vivid memory of those innocent days. The precious two weeks every other year in a broken-down cottage at the shore. Few comforts, but it was only a short walk to the white sandy beach. There were slippery rocks to climb over at low tide and little crabs and snails to discover in the tidal pools. The sea was unpolluted, and there was always a fish at the end of the line. Her father took her with him when he bought the lobsters with glaring eyes and wooden pegs in their claws from the old lobsterman who lived down the road. Sometimes her cousin Rita came down from the city for a week, and they'd giggle and whisper about what excitement the future promised.

"The beaches were clean when I was a child. But that was long ago," she said shortly, "before the war, before you were born."

CHAPTER 14

"EXACTLY WHAT is it you've been doing between the Second World War and now?" Ted was watching her expectantly. He'd inputted the items she'd given him on his laptop, but now he placed the little computer aside.

"I'd rather not discuss the past," Betty said. He was too curious for her taste. "Is there anything else I can do? I'm here to have dinner and report on events at Zig-Zag, not my life story."

"Sorry," he said. "I understand about privacy. The potatoes are baked, the spinach is creamed, and the butter is melted."

She relaxed and sniffed the air. "There's something else."

"Apple pie, sweetened with my own honey."

"They told me about the bees."

"They?"

"Marsha at Zig-Zag, actually. Your helper's wife. Penny Saks."

"I hate knowing they talk about me," he said, "but I know they must. They're talking about you, too. That limo must have set tongues wagging."

"I told you it was only Mr. Mitsui." She was uncomfortable under his questioning look.

"Only Mr. Mitsui. Hmm," he said after a moment. "We'll get to your association with Mr. Mitsui. Anything else about these murders?"

"This young girl, Eve, so strongly denied being the late-night witness to Denise's death," Betty said, "but I didn't believe her. Today I discovered that she's run away. Or . . . I worry that the murderer knew about her."

Ted nodded. "Eve used to baby-sit the Saks boys, and I know her from the produce stand. Like a lot of healthy young people, she was uncomfortable being confronted with my physical disabilities. Have you taken it upon yourself to inform the police of the possibility that Eve saw something? Or that she's missing?"

"I haven't," Betty said. "Her mother hasn't. I suppose I should, but I don't want to intrude."

Ted reached for the telephone. "I have no such qualms." He dialed a number and spoke for a minute, then hung up. "Our trooper will call me back," he said.

She said, "Eve told me that Alan Brown supposedly found Denise's body early in the morning when he was out running. What about him? People say—"

"People say all sorts of things," he said, rather more abruptly than necessary. "Alan and Denise were an item some years ago, when May–late September romances were not acceptable, especially not to Mrs. Brown. It was over long ago. Long ago," he repeated.

Betty wondered if that was so. He had the sound of a jealous man. She chose not to ask if besides the Nicole-Alan-Denise triangle that was the "usual small-town stuff," long forgotten, there had been another: Alan-Denise-Ted.

"He lives with his mother, I understand," she said, "who didn't like Denise."

"You are surprisingly well informed for a newcomer, but don't start suspecting Mrs. Brown. She has a notorious mean streak and is pathologically proud of her standing in the town, but I doubt she'd stoop to murdering Denise. And there's no connection with Amanda. There has to be one."

Betty said tentatively, "Both of them were on foot at some point. Both were struck. Amanda was sitting at Denise's desk in the chair where she wanted to be permanently, probably meeting someone she knew. Denise was out walking, probably meeting someone she trusted but who perhaps couldn't be seen coming to her house. Alan Brown?"

"Him again." Ted shrugged. "I've never gotten on with him, but I don't see him as a murderer. What about Mitsui? Ah!" He looked at her expectantly. "You're holding something back, Elizabeth. Tell me. It could be important."

She hesitated. Should she speak about Mr. Mitsui now? He'd claimed Denise had been acting on his behalf. He'd been found by Betty with Amanda's body. He'd worked with Denise; he'd known Amanda in passing. Still, she wasn't sure whether she should speak of those matters.

Then she asked herself, Does it matter, after all, if Ted or the whole world knows what Denise had been doing? She felt tired, more tired than she had ever been during crises at Edwards & Son. She sighed. "All right. There is something," Betty said slowly. "I haven't told anyone else." Ted leaned forward and watched her. "Denise was supposedly an agent for Mr. Mitsui's organization. She 'represented our interests,' according to him. And she was the one who introduced Mr. Mitsui to Zig-Zag, although it's not clear if Jerry Preston realized that."

"So that's it. I suspected something. And did he come around trying to recruit you now that she's no longer available?"

"I told you he thinks I am more important than I am. But yes. I refused. Naturally. There's more. I came upon Mr. Mitsui looking at Amanda's body. He fled before the police came and I didn't tell them. He did, though—later. He actually told them he'd noticed her from the hall, but I came upon him standing over her body in Denise's office. He couldn't have done it—not right then—but I can't help wondering what he was doing in that office."

"Looking for something, or making sure Amanda was dead?"

"Do you think so?" Betty thought for a moment. "You could be right. He might have been looking for something like papers that would link him and Denise. But no.

Mr. Mitsui told me the arrangement had died with her. Nothing on paper was the suggestion."

"Then I wonder who benefits by these deaths. Does he? Someone else? Elizabeth, why don't you accept Mitsui's offer? You could find some answers and he probably pays well, if Denise is any example. She was able to afford almost anything, and now I have to assume it came from Mitsui's organization."

"I couldn't. Absolutely not."

"Then at least give him the opportunity to convince you. It might give you an idea of what the arrangements were with Zig-Zag, what he was after."

"The new software. Mitsui and Denise." Betty shook her head. "Company loyalty doesn't seem to have been one of Denise's shining qualities."

"Denise was okay, but she liked to look out for herself." Ted looked at his watch. "Time to take those lobsters out. I could do it, but as long as you're here . . ."

"You're good at having people handle things," Betty said with complete good humor.

"Yes," he said, "and why not? I don't want boiling water in my lap, so I reduce the chances. Once you dump them on the counter, I'll crack the claws and put the rest of the dinner on the table. No, I don't want more help. Take a seat at the table and let me think a minute."

He put the baked potatoes and a bowl of sour cream on the table, then brought the cracked lobsters and the rest of the food on a rolling cart.

"Too much cholesterol for two people, but I don't do this kind of meal too often," he said. "About Nicole Preston. She drove up in a rage because Jerry hadn't picked her up, looked around, opened his office door, closed, it, and left?"

"Correct."

He dipped a chunk of lobster meat into the butter. "Could Preston's wife have seen Amanda lying in Denise's office but left without saying anything to you?"

"Not impossible, I suppose. I should say that Nicole Preston told me she'd have me fired if I mentioned her presence to the police. Since I already had, and since I fortunately do not really work at Zig-Zag, it was an empty threat. According to Amanda when I met her that first day, Nicole didn't like her. Perhaps because of this . . . this rumored romance you mentioned. Nicole could have been delighted to see her dead."

"Delicately put," Ted said, "but I don't think even a highly impulsive woman would slaughter another simply because of a passing indiscretion. George Hammond, however, is something else. Locally he has a reputation as a fearsome businessman, but I don't know how true that is. That office park is not a resounding success. On the other hand, Zig-Zag could be."

Betty shook her head. "He seems always on the verge of exploding. And he is constantly rude to the help." The chunks of lobster pulled from the shell were sweet and tender, the potatoes hot and fluffy, the spinach faintly tinged with nutmeg.

The phone rang, and Ted moved away to answer it. Betty examined the possibility that Jerry Preston had somehow discovered that Denise, his right-hand woman, was conniving with the Japanese and had taken a radical step to stop it. Then, if Amanda knew—or thought she knew—something about Denise's death and had tried blackmailing him to give her Denise's place, eliminating Amanda would have stopped that threat. Logical, but was it the way things had happened?

"The police are aware that Eve has run away," Ted said after he hung up the phone. "Her mother finally called them. They find your tale that she might have seen something when Denise died rather thin. A resident of the neighborhood happened to look out her window late that night and saw a car stop at the bridge and then go on. She didn't actually see anyone get run over or anyone bashing poor Denise."

"Eve was frightened, I'm certain of that," Betty said. She felt hopeless. "We've done our best."

"Not at all," he said. "Not yet. Are you ready to try my pie before we decide on the next step?"

"You enjoy cooking," she said. She didn't like the sound of "the next step." She'd done what he'd asked.

"When I was in therapy, they tried to interest me in all kinds of things," Ted said. "Cooking won out as a peaceful indoor recreation,"

"What is it that you do otherwise?" Betty asked with some trepidation. He hadn't volunteered anything, and she thought he might tell her to mind her own business as readily as she had told him.

"Research," he said. "I never fail to be amazed by how computers can link you up with all kinds of information that you can then put together and come up with something else. Dial tone," he said, "is one of the great miracles of our time. It enables you to find answers."

"Rather what we're doing now," Betty said. He hadn't really told her anything about himself. Well, it was none of her business.

"Except you haven't come up with anything," Ted said. "Try harder."

"Me? I'm not a crime solver. And you're the one who puts things together and comes up with answers."

"Not in this situation. I want to know, but I'm not going to be the agent of justice. I'm merely curious."

Betty put down her fork. She hoped he recognized her annoyance. "So I'm here just to satisfy your curiosity." She pushed away from the table. She was ready to stand up and leave.

"Calm down, Elizabeth. Consider this. Maybe Amanda did find something. Maybe she was a blackmailer, say—"

"Marsha did say she was nosy. I took it to mean she wanted to know things in order to better her standing with Jerry. But if she was blackmailing Denise because she knew something or even blackmailing Mr. Mitsui . . ."

"I retract my suggestion," Ted said. "Blackmail is such a childish way to make money."

"I wouldn't say that Amanda got high grades for maturity," Betty said, but she was turning the idea of blackmail over in her mind.

"I'll bet Mitsui corners you again," he said. "See if he tells you anything. No, don't worry about the dishes. I have a dishwasher. In spite of everything, I can handle most things. Just like you."

"Me?"

"We both have our handicaps, Elizabeth. Yours aren't so obvious. This isn't a society devoted to its disabled or its aging or its otherwise disadvantaged. We have to fight our way all the time. We have to handle things."

"You're lecturing me on attitude," Betty said.

"In a way. You have to look at what you have rather than what you don't have. Right now you and I have our lives, and Amanda and Denise don't." He looked momentarily stricken. He'd been fonder of Denise than he admitted.

"Death as the ultimate handicap?"

"Exactly. God, I'm going to miss her. We talked by phone or through the computer every day, messages in our electronic mailboxes, that sort of thing. I wonder . . ." He wheeled himself over to a PC, turned it on, and selected a screen from the menu. "I haven't looked at this since I heard she was dead early Saturday. She was all keyed up at dinner, not really herself. She usually told me everything about Zig-Zag—well, almost everything, as you have indicated. She was holding back something at dinner, as though she wanted to surprise me when the time was right. I assumed it had to do with her business at Zig-Zag. Ah!"

There was indeed a message from Denise, short and surprising, which she had sent to Ted's mailbox after their dinner on Friday and before she'd gone out to meet her death. It was not, however, about her business at Zig-Zag.

"I'll be in New York by the time you read this," the message said. "I couldn't bear to tell you face-to-face. Alan and I have decided to get married when things are settled with Mitsui. I hope you'll be happy for me. Don't spend the weekend piling up arguments about the difference in age.

I'll be home on Tuesday and we'll talk. Face-to-face, I promise. Love, D."

"Idiot!" The tension in his voice signified deep shock. "How can she?"

"She can't," Betty said. "She's dead."

Ted stared at the screen for a long time. Then he said briskly, "You're right. No more grief, no regrets." He looked at Betty. "I was never in love with Denise, but I thought of the two of us as a couple of some sort. Do you understand what I mean?"

She nodded. She understood very well.

"Her death was bad enough, a kind of betrayal that nobody can do anything about. But this . . ." He gestured toward the blank screen. "This was done while she was alive." He was silent for a moment. "Perhaps she didn't realize how much it would hurt."

He probably wouldn't welcome sympathetic words, Betty thought, so she merely nodded again. Her lack of comment seemed to bring him around from his moment of pain at the double betrayal by Denise: her marriage plans and her death.

"I'm Denise's executor," he said. "The good and trusted friend." This was added with a touch of bitterness. "I've done the funeral and seen the lawyer," he went on, "and now I have to go over to her house tomorrow to start to organize things. Would you care to come by after work?"

"With more of my discoveries at Zig-Zag?"

"If there are any. Who knows what I'll discover at Denise's place? And I think you should talk with Alan Brown."

"Me? What would I say?"

"See what his mood is," Ted said. Then, almost savagely, "Find out if he killed her. I couldn't talk to him now, not after this." He waved at the computer. "You could arrange to encounter him while he's out running tomorrow morning. And see if you can find out anything more about Eve's whereabouts from her mother. Then when you get to Zig-Zag, get what you can from Jerry Preston. Did it occur to you that Jerry might have confessed doing the awful deed to Amanda and then sent his wife to make sure she was dead?"

"Aren't the police supposed to do this? You said you're not an agent of justice," Betty said.

"No, I'm not," he said hastily, "but I feel I have to know. As long as you're here, could you pile the dishes beside the sink? Then we'll just go over again what it is you should be looking and listening for. I have to figure this out. We have to."

Betty had the sense that she was not, after all, entirely alone and on her own.

CHAPTER 15

THE ALARM woke Betty before dawn.

She lay in bed for a time thinking about her evening with Ted Kelso. There was something they'd touched on but had let pass, and that was the matter of blackmail. Amanda might have thought it a clever way to achieve power, but there was another person who might have seen it as an opportunity to gratify longings that couldn't be satisfied in a town like East Moulton. If Eve had recognized the person at the bridge and decided to try blackmail . . .

Betty prayed that the police would find her, that she wasn't also lying dead in the woods. She would talk to Alan Brown for Ted's sake, but then she would speak again with Eve's mother.

She and Ted had decided that no one would go running much before six, so she planned to be somewhere on Prospect Street well before that hour. If Alan Brown and his retriever were out, she'd see them.

Ted had been very determined that she speak to Alan. "I can't believe he did it, but you have to get a reading on him."

She had no idea how she'd approach Alan Brown. She was a stranger to him and very nearly a contemporary of his mother's. She wondered if he would see her as a dominating mother figure and choose not to speak to her at all.

A new weather front had brought in a light fog that lay near the ground, so only the tops of the trees rose above it. It was thick enough to make ground-level visibility difficult. Betty dressed for another day at Zig-Zag—probably her last—and drove very carefully. The few oncoming cars had their headlights on, pale yellowish circles that cast little light in the fog.

She was especially careful as she drove the hills and curves of Prospect Street. There were no other cars here, and no sight of Alan and his dog running along the grassy edge of the road.

Betty reached the bridge over the little stream and pulled her car off the road onto the patch of gravel. She rolled down the window and listened again to the sound of the water in the brook. Other than that sound, it was eerily silent. She got out of the car and walked to the middle of the bridge through the damp mist.

She raised her head and listened. She thought she heard a faint but steady footfall, as though someone was running along the gravel at the edge of the road. Then she heard a faint jingle and the golden retriever emerged from the fog, its tongue lolling as it loped along the roadside. Not far behind a man in running shorts and a windbreaker was visible.

The dog noticed her as soon as she noticed it. It stopped short and raised its platinum muzzle in her direction.

"Good dog," she said hopefully. It was a handsome animal but rather large.

The man—it was the same person she had seen with Mrs. Brown in the supermarket—slowed his run and stopped beside Betty on the bridge.

"Stay, Buddy," the man said. "Are you having a problem with the car?" His voice was soft, as if muffled by the fog. He was what used to be called "presentable," although not robust, and he still looked sad. That was more understandable now, since he'd lost a bride to murder.

"No," she said. "The car's all right. Mr. Brown?"

He looked startled to be addressed by name by a strange woman.

"I'm Elizabeth Trenka. I just moved to East Moulton. I met your mother on Sunday. . . ."

Now he seemed puzzled to discover an acquaintance of

his mother's in this unlikely spot. "She doesn't receive visitors until later," he said. "You should call on her after ten. Nice meeting you. Come, Buddy." The dog was poised to continue the run.

"Actually, I wanted to speak to you," Betty said. This was unfamiliar territory for her, questioning a person even tangentially involved in a murder.

"Me?"

"About Denise Legrand."

He started back as though she had transformed herself from a pleasant older lady, nicely dressed in a tweedy suit and sensible flats, into a raging dragon with fire spouting from her nostrils.

"There's nothing to say. She's dead," he said. "Dead." He backed away from her.

"I heard that you found her," Betty said. "That must have been a terrible shock. It would have been just about here, where we're standing."

He was beginning to look desperate. She thought he would simply start running into the gray fog and not stop until he was far beyond her reach.

"I've told the police everything I know. There's nothing to add. She was lying there by the bridge, off the road."

Now he did move away resolutely while the dog awaited his signal to run. Betty didn't want him to leave yet. Ted thought she should try to learn if Alan had been in the habit of meeting Denise along this road through the many years since that old town scandal involving the two of them. Betty had argued that he wouldn't admit to it, not with a murder involved, but Ted had insisted. She decided her only chance with Alan was to be firm and sensible.

"Mr. Brown, I know this is upsetting, and I'm not simply a sensation seeker. I work at Zig-Zag . . ." Barely true, but never mind. "Her death has upset us, and we need to understand."

"I hadn't spoken to Denise in weeks . . . months."

"Yet you live on the same street. You must have met, if

only by accident." Betty thought he was beginning to look haunted.

"That isn't true," he said. "If you think you can get on my mother's good side by spreading gossip—"

"I am not a friend of your mother's," she said quickly. "I'm not going to share anything with her, but surely in a small town like East Moulton, on a street like this where you run with your dog, you had occasion to see Denise. Perhaps people have seen you together under perfectly innocent circumstances and remembered that you and she were once close and assumed you still were." Indeed, Amanda had practically told her about Denise and Alan. Amanda had seen her with a "boyfriend" from East Moulton when they hadn't known she was around. "Did the police ask you if you'd seen her the night she died?"

He gave up. "They did. They asked all the neighbors. I . . . We did meet here on the road at night. I almost never went to her house." His eyes flickered toward his own house on the hill. "We occasionally met at parties in the area, although she didn't socialize much in this town. We reestablished our . . . friendship after she came back to East Moulton, but when we did go out, it was to places in New Haven or Hartford. It was just a casual friendship."

"But I understood you were planning to marry."

Alan Brown looked alarmed. "Who told you that?"

"Denise herself," Betty said. "She left a message for Ted Kelso."

"It's not so," he said vehemently. "Denise wanted . . . she always wanted to marry me. But it wasn't possible back then, and it wasn't possible now. She might have gotten the idea that maybe someday . . . I couldn't leave my mother. Denise wanted everything. Look, I can't let people around here know about all this. You know how they talk."

Betty sighed inwardly. It was so hard to have everything. It was harder still to keep people from talking. "Did she speak much about her business affairs?"

"Not a lot. She was doing very well, though. Jerry

thought highly of her. She stood to do very well from some deal she was involved in."

"You do know the Prestons, of course. Is that how you came to suggest to Nicole that Jerry hire Denise as his assistant?"

"There was nothing in that. I've know Nicole since we were kids, so naturally I know him. Denise was looking for a job after she came back, and I mentioned it to Nicole. They'd never been friendly, but Denise had a good head for business."

"Could you tell me about finding her, if it doesn't distress you too much?"

"I just found her lying there off the road near the bridge. At first I thought she'd fainted. Then I saw that she was dead. I went right back to our house and called the police. They came and said it was a hit-and-run."

"It wasn't," Betty said. "She was murdered."

Alan looked at her without speaking.

"You knew?" she asked.

"Yes. The police asked me not to say anything just then."

"I see. Why would she have been walking alone late at night, do you suppose?"

"I suppose," Alan said grimly, "that she had an appointment."

"With someone who killed her?"

"You'd have to ask the police. It wasn't me." He turned his back on her, whistled, and started to run back up the hill the way he'd come. The retriever followed joyfully at his heels.

"Wait!" Betty called out. "Eve. Evelyn. You do know her, don't you?"

Alan stopped. "Yes. From the farm. What about her?"

"She's run away."

"Denise said it was bound to happen. Tough family life." He looked as though he sympathized with that. "I helped her get a couple of jobs baby-sitting for friends. Nicole and

Jerry; some others over in Hodders Woods. She wanted to earn money, probably to get away, poor kid."

"When you were out at night on this road, did you ever see Eve?"

"No." He spoke too quickly to convince Betty. She waited. "Well, once or twice I saw her walking with a boy. I promised her I wouldn't tell her father. I've got to get going."

He was running again, and after a few seconds man and dog were dim figures in the fog.

Betty watched them. He and Denise had met often to keep their old romance in flower, but secretly so that the formidable mother wouldn't see them, where the gossipy neighbors weren't likely to be. If there really had been marriage plans, he'd naturally deny them now.

Nothing was any clearer, in her mind or on the foggy road, as she drove the short distance to Eve's house. She could make out Eve's mother walking toward the barn. Betty pulled into the wide dirt circle in front of the produce stand. A few early pumpkins had been piled on the ground, but the stand was empty otherwise. Eve's mother looked back at the sound of the car. She hesitated. Betty waved and started to walk toward her.

"I wondered if there was news of Eve," Betty said.

The woman didn't smile or frown. Betty wondered if she even recognized her.

"We won't be seeing her again, that's what her father says. I told the police she'd gone, but they say she's run away like a lot of these kids do. It was bound to happen. I found a note. Said not to worry, she'd have money to take care of herself."

Betty didn't know what to say. A note showed she'd gone of her own accord, but she couldn't tell Eve's mother that she might also be running from perceived or real danger, if she'd actually seen a murder committed.

"I hope you'll let me know if she turns up," Betty said. She took out her pocket notebook and wrote out the new telephone number she'd managed to memorize. "I don't suppose she regularly went out at night, did she?"

"Her father wouldn't hear of it," Eve's mother said quickly. "She only went to school dances when he could drive her and pick her up. She did some baby-sitting for these rich women who don't want to stay at home with their kids. Evie was good with kids. The parents picked her up and brought her home."

"She didn't go out at night otherwise, then."

"I said not," the woman said, but she looked away guiltily as though she was making sure the strict father wasn't listening. The mother seemed well aware that her daughter had sometimes sneaked away from the house after dark to meet a boyfriend in the fields or beside the brook. Or she'd get into the car of a friend waiting somewhere on dark Prospect Street and drive down the highway to the nearest disco and come home undetected.

"Don't worry," Betty said. "I'm sure she's all right. Young people today do the wildest things."

"Small comfort," Eve's mother said. "I'm worried sick. She didn't take anything but what she was wearing as far as I can tell."

"I wonder. Did she have a boyfriend? I mean, someone who's also missing?"

"All the kids are accounted for," Eve's mother said. "That's worse. She went on her own."

CHAPTER 16

"On her own."

Indeed she is, Betty thought as she drove away from the farm. It was still far too early to go to Zig-Zag, where she had nothing to do, in any case, except possibly pick up a very modest check for a couple of days of work, such as it had been. It seemed pointless to return home for an hour and then set out again.

Then she remembered the key. She'd never had a chance to return it to Reuben. She'd even forgotten to mention that she had it to Ted Kelso. Just as well. He would have had her at Zig-Zag at dawn to do a search of the place.

It would still be early if she went to Zig-Zag now and . . . She stopped herself. She was *not* going to rifle the files or search Denise's desk. In any case, she assumed that Denise's office would still be off-limits, but she might be able to stand in the doorway and refresh her memory of it and the scene of Amanda's death.

When she reached Main Street, she was undecided about whether to stop at the drugstore to chat with Molly Perkins and perhaps pick up some gossipy tidbit of value or to turn in the opposite direction to reach Hammond Center and Zig-Zag.

Molly won. The excuse would be aspirin.

"Bright and early, Miz Trenka—Elizabeth, I should say." Molly was at her post behind the counter in the store. Betty was the only customer. "Just got here myself. We like to open early for folks on their way to work. What's this I

hear about a gentleman in a limousine? Japanese, they say."
Molly waited expectantly.

"A business matter," Betty said. Word did spread fast in
this town.

"And this poor girl murdered over in Hammond Center."
Now Molly was looking extremely hopeful. "I hear you—"

"I happen to be working temporarily at her office," Betty
said quickly. There was no way she could get around this.
If she said nothing, Molly would contrive three juicy, spec-
ulative paragraphs. If she said anything but the plain truth,
it would get distorted beyond recognition. Even the plain
truth, however, wasn't likely to fare any better.

"It must have been just terrible. Who could have done
such a thing?"

"I'm sure the police will discover the guilty party," Betty
said.

"That top-secret stuff is dangerous. Spies and things."

"I'm sure it has nothing to do with the business," Betty
said. "They say most violent crimes involve people who
know each other, and it's some personal matter."

Molly looked doubtful. Then she said, "It's plain to me.
Two people from the same company dead."

"Denise's was an accident," Betty said, knowing it was
not.

"That's what they *said*. Poor Alan found her body. I just
heard that one."

Betty had at least been saved from facing the problem of
how to get around to Alan Brown.

"I've never entirely understood about Alan Brown and
Denise," Betty said, the actual fact being that she knew
quite a bit, probably more than Molly Perkins.

"Years ago it was," Molly said. "Denise grew up in this
part of the world and got mixed up with Alan when he
came back home from law school. He was in his twenties
then, and she was a good ten years older. They were actually planning to get married. Alma, that's Miz Brown,
wouldn't hear of it. Said Denise was after old Mr. Brown's
money. The truth is, Denise wasn't in the same class as the

Browns, if you get my meaning. And she was older. I guess that was one case where the apron strings won out."

"The Browns are well off, then?" A fact not conveyed by Ted Kelso.

"Yes and no," Molly said. "Alma acts as though they are. Mr. Brown was in business for a time with George Hammond. We always heard he did very well from it, but he's been gone for years."

"Didn't I hear that the Hammonds have lived around here for a long time?"

"Oh, yes. Now they *are* very well off. Alma Brown hoped for years that Alan would settle down with the Hammond girl, but no. When the thing with Denise got broken off, he just sort of sat there while she went off to work for some fancy company with offices all over the world."

"Really. How interesting that must have been." Out in the world of big business Denise would have met people like Mr. Mitsui.

"Just think, after all these years, Denise was working at the place run by the man the Hammond girl married."

"Such a small world," Betty said. "I'll take this aspirin."

"Do you have trouble with headaches, Elizabeth?"

"Only occasionally," Betty said. "I feel one coming on."

She drove to Zig-Zag thinking about the amazing connections between people in towns like this. For the moment, however, her main concerns were with what the day at Zig-Zag would hold and whether Mr. Mitsui would continue his pursuit of her. She thought he must be keeping track of her in case she was inclined to tell a detailed story of his presence at Zig-Zag to the police.

It was still too early for Eileen and the others to have arrived at Zig-Zag. That explained the empty parking lot. The early hour alone, however, did not explain the look of closed-in desolation that seemed to emanate from the building. Then Betty realized that all of the blinds had been lowered over the windows. She supposed that one of Reuben's daily tasks was to raise them.

As she approached the front door, with Reuben's key in hand, she noticed a sheet of paper taped on the glass. When she was a few yards from the door, the large handprinted letters were clear: CLOSED.

Closed? One didn't simply "close" a company overnight. She peered through her glasses at the smaller printing beneath the closed notice. UNTIL FURTHER NOTICE. Nothing else, no name to indicate by whose authority Zig-Zag had been shut down. She didn't see a police seal on the door, so Zig-Zag was not officially closed because of the murder.

Betty looked at the key in her hand, then inserted it into the lock. The door swung open. At least no one had changed the lock when the offices of Zig-Zag Incorporated were closed.

She entered the silent, darkened reception area and listened. Not a sound anywhere. She decided not to turn on the overhead lights. First she ventured down the hallway in the direction of the accounting room and the copier. Nothing to be seen.

Down the other corridor she found that some of the offices had boxes piled on the floor with the drawers of filing cabinets open and empty. Denise's office was still much as she'd first seen it. She didn't enter but stood in the doorway. She turned on the overhead lights. They flickered and then lit up. A dusting of powder covered the desk and other furnishings, probably the result of police tests for fingerprints.

A white outline on the floor marked the shape of Amanda's body. She could see the body again in her mind's eye and didn't like it. Bits of dirt from the ceramic planter remained on the carpet, and a spot of Amanda's dried blood, but the pot itself was gone. Denise's other plants still stood on the table in front of the window, though there was a gap where the pot that had killed Amanda had been taken.

Betty closed her eyes and tried to imagine a person entering the office to find Amanda Glyn sitting behind the desk, waiting. She imagined a display of arrogant assurance—easy enough to imagine, since she'd experienced it herself. Then she imagined two people facing each other and Amanda overstepping herself in her triumph at being within reach of her goal by virtue of Denise's death.

She had probably thought she was acting from a position of strength. Indeed, she'd asked Betty if Mitsui had sent her, which suggested that she had known something about the relationship between Denise and Mr. Mitsui. Betty imagined how the person Amanda was meeting had been roused to anger by her presumption, had moved to the table of plants, had quickly raised the heavy ceramic pot.

Betty had known a lot of girls like Amanda over the years. Capable but unwise, believing they knew everything, when in fact they were merely minor cogs in the wheels of business.

She thought back to Tuesday morning as she had sat alone at Zig-Zag and seen the arrival of Nicole, Mr. Mitsui, George Hammond, and finally Jerry and the staff.

One of them had been there earlier and had left Amanda lying dead. One of them had been on Prospect Street late at night and had ended Denise's life.

She felt indignation rising at the waste of two women's lives.

"What the hell's going on here?"

The unmistakable voice of George Hammond rumbled through the empty building.

Betty could hear him stamping along the corridor and caught a glimpse of the lights flickering on along the corridor. "I'm in here," she said. She thought he might react unpredictably and possibly violently at being surprised under these circumstances. She met him in the corridor.

"Who are you?"

"Elizabeth Trenka," she said. Apparently it was necessary to reintroduce oneself to George Hammond at every meeting. "I work here."

"You've got no business here. The place is closed."

"The door was open," Betty lied. "I thought the sign was

just for customers." She decided she wanted to hang on to the key.

"Then they forgot to call you. I had Caruso and Jerry in here to clear things up. There's no more work for any of you girls."

"Never? It's closed for good?" Betty didn't mind being called a girl by the other "girls," but she disliked being condescended to by a man who was probably her own age. And very likely younger.

"Don't you hear well? Zig-Zag is closed."

"What about all the people who work here?"

Hammond dismissed them. "Everybody gets paid and then they'll have unemployment."

"What about me? I didn't get paid," Betty said. Now she was feeling stubborn as well as indignant. She didn't like his attitude. However, she didn't wish to put herself entirely on his bad side at this point. "I'm not on the official payroll."

Hammond look exasperated. He glanced at his watch and started back toward the reception area. "Then go over to Jerry's place and have him pay you," he said over his shoulder. "He's probably at home. They're over in Hodders Woods. Know where that is?"

She nodded. She had a rough idea. She'd find it.

"Tell him I said to pay you off. Then don't come back."

"I understand," Betty said as ingratiatingly as she could. "Thank you so much, Mr. Hammond."

He calmed down, and as she started to leave, Mr. Mitsui's limousine glided to a stop in front of the building.

"Here's Mr. Mitsui to see you," she said over her shoulder to Hammond.

"The Jap? How do you know him?" He was suspicious and surly again.

"One gets to know all sorts of people in the business world," Betty said sweetly.

Mr. Mitsui was descending from his limousine. She thought fast and was quickly out of the building and at his side.

"Good morning, Mr. Mitsui. I have been reconsidering your offer . . ."

Mr. Mitsui bowed to her, quite deeply this time. "I would be glad to discuss this matter, Miss Trenka. You will be free to dine with me tonight?"

She knew George Hammond was watching from the building. She bowed to Mr. Mitsui very, very slightly.

"I would be happy to."

Mr. Mitsui bowed again. It seemed that she and Mr. Mitsui were now formally engaged professionally.

"My driver will be at your house at seven."

Another round of gossip for the neighborhood, she thought, then said, "Excellent. May I request that you not discuss our association with Mr. Hammond? I believe I understand what your business with Zig-Zag is."

He nodded. "A woman of wisdom, as I stated."

Considerable wisdom, if I do say so myself, she thought, and I still have the key to Zig-Zag. More than that, from her visit to Denise's office, she thought she understood now who it must have been that Amanda had faced. She knew now who Eve must have seen the night Denise died.

CHAPTER 17

BETTY STOOD in the parking lot of Zig-Zag Incorporated as Mr. Mitsui disappeared through the main door. She caught a glimpse of a jovial George Hammond wrapping a hefty and comradely arm around the much-shorter man's shoulder and hustling him into the depths of the building. Negotiations were apparently to proceed without Denise—and without Jerry Preston.

She thought about her sudden illumination in Denise's office. She was so sure she knew the answer to the murders, but there was no proof except her understanding of the way things worked in offices. She did not know what she should do about it.

Mr. Mitsui's limousine was parked at the far side of the lot. The uniformed driver was polishing the spotless hood. He flicked a last mote of invisible dust from the windshield and got into the driver's seat. The smoked-glass window glided upward and the engine started. Instead of departing via the main drive down the incline and past the handful of other office buildings in grassy settings, the limo took a hitherto undetected driveway behind the Zig-Zag building and disappeared.

Betty thought for a moment. A back way. A service road. The programmer's entrance was in the back of the building. She couldn't risk going on foot to explore it, since George Hammond and Mr. Mitsui were in one of the offices. Although she couldn't see in because of the lowered blinds, they might be able to see out. She didn't want to be caught snooping. She got into her car.

The service road behind the Zig-Zag building dipped sharply, so that the view of the gentle landscaped hills from the windows would not be contaminated by the sight of a roadway. At the bottom of the dip was a line of big green covered plastic trash barrels standing near a tall, wide door for a garage or loading dock. Next to the doorway was an ordinary steel door set in windowless concrete. At this point, because of the hill on which it was built, the Zig-Zag building loomed a story above the service road, which continued on toward the next building of the office park some distance away.

Betty stopped her car near the back door. She didn't think anyone in the building above would see it unless he or she made a point of standing close to the window and looking down.

The steel door was locked, but when Betty examined the lock, she found that it appeared to be the same sort as the one for the main door. She did not hesitate to use Reuben's key, and she was not much surprised when the door opened.

Before her stretched a hall with cement-block walls painted a greenish white. The line of fluorescent lights on the low ceiling was on. The evenly spaced doors on either side were closed, except for the one near the end of the hallway where she could see the stairs going up to the main floor. Betty made her way cautiously toward the open door.

The room she entered was lined with computer screens and other hardware. There were a couple of phones and some devices she recognized as modems. One of the two programmers she'd seen earlier was sitting in an old-fashioned wooden desk chair with a rounded back and curving arms. The other was standing beside him. They were both intently watching a computer screen.

It was a room with no windows and no distractions, a place where you could concentrate entirely on putting together pieces of an electronic puzzle. She could imagine Jerry Preston sitting here finding his "cure."

"Pardon me," Betty said, not too loudly lest she startle

them. She did not. Slowly and reluctantly they took their eyes off the screen and turned toward her. "I don't mean to interrupt, but since no one is in the office today . . ."

One of the programmers looked at his watch. "It's only seven-forty-five."

"So it is, I'd forgotten how early it was. What I meant to say is, since Zig-Zag is closed until further notice . . ."

The two men looked at each other. They had put aside the jackets and ties they had worn yesterday and were back in jeans and T-shirts. One wore an unbuttoned plaid shirt over his T-shirt. In his pocket was a row of pens in a plastic holder. The other wore his hair in a tasteful ponytail.

"Closed?" They spoke in unison.

"Ah, you probably didn't notice, if you came in by the back door this morning. But Mr. Hammond said they'd called everyone."

"We didn't notice because we've been here since eight last night," one said, "and nobody called us. We were just about to leave for the day."

"I understood Jerry and Mr. Caruso and Mr. Hammond were clearing things up in the office last night," Betty said.

"Nobody came down here."

"Are you here every night?" she asked. She understood about flex time, but this seemed to be extreme.

They looked at each other again, as though trying to determine the correct answer.

"Not every night," said the one with the plaid shirt.

"What about Monday night when Miss Glyn was killed?"

"The police asked us that," said the other man. "We both left at nine because we had come in early. Jerry wanted us to be around for that meeting about Denise. Waste of time. Nobody is likely to ask us anything about her."

"I'm asking."

"You work here." A perfectly logical statement from Plaid Shirt. "We had to be around early on Tuesday morning, too, for Denise's funeral."

"I see. I don't suppose that Jerry was around on Monday night."

"Not when we were here," said Plaid Shirt. "But he was here sometime that night after we left. We can always tell when he's dropped by to fool around or look at our stuff."

"I suppose there's no way of telling how late Jerry was here on Monday," Betty said.

"Late. Early, rather. He logged out at three in the morning. It was already Tuesday. I know because he left us some notes."

"Did you mention that to the police?"

The two looked at each other once more and shrugged. "Yeah." Again this was in unison.

"Hey, Jerry's okay, you know?" Plaid Shirt said. "He doesn't go around killing people, if that's what you're thinking. He's a computer guy. He loves his wife and his kid and software." The other one nodded at every word.

She was beginning to think of them as the microchip twins. Although they looked nothing alike on the outside, they seemed to think identically.

"Amanda was sort of after him, you know? Even we noticed it. But he laughed it off. Nicole is enough to handle."

"Oh?"

The two men looked at each other again.

"Jerry loves this company, all the work we're doing. Great stuff," Plaid Shirt said. They looked at each other again. "Nicole resents him hanging out here in the programming room. I've heard his side anyhow, when she's called him here," he added carefully. "Look, we want to get going."

"Of course," Betty said. "Just one more question. I'm curious about whether the same key I used opens the door upstairs into the offices."

"Yeah. I don't think anybody's ever caught on about that. Jerry knows, but none of the girls ever needs to be here." He made it sound as though the room was off-limits to women.

The other one grinned. "We made it a point to chase Denise and Mrs. P. away the couple times they thought they'd look the place over. Amanda got as far as the back door once. We don't need those interruptions."

"Then I'd better join the parade of ladies out of here," Betty said. ""How do you get here?"

"Get here?" Plaid Shirt chuckled. "I'll bet the answer isn't practice, practice, practice. Are you asking where our cars are?" She nodded. "They're in the garage next door. It was designed for shipping, but it's not used for that."

"Jerry is one smart dude," the other said. "I wish he were still working full time with us."

"He may be soon," Betty said, "if Zig-Zag is closed."

"What are we supposed to do now?" Plaid Shirt said. "It's not fair to put us out of work just like that."

"I know," she said grimly. "It may just be temporary," she added, although she didn't believe it. "I'll ask Jerry. I have to see him." The least of Betty's worries was the undoubtedly negligible wages she had earned in two days.

"Ask him, will you? We're finishing something important for him."

"I know," Betty said.

They looked at her doubtfully. "It's supposed to be secret," Ponytail said.

"I'm afraid several people know," she said. "Denise probably even took a copy of the new software—"

"Hey, don't get us in trouble about that. We had no choice. The source code's safe." But they looked uneasy.

"I won't mention any of this," Betty said.

"Have Jerry give us a call, would you? I'd sure hate to stop what I'm on, but I'll have to look around if this place is finished." He shrugged. "I thought the economy was improving."

"It may be," Betty said, but she was thinking that it was probably improving for George Hammond or whoever owned Zig-Zag and could cash Mr. Mitsui's check.

Her next problem was to find Jerry Preston's home in the new Hodders Woods development.

The problem of his address was solved efficiently by borrowing a telephone book from the clerk in a not-thriving shoe store in the minimall. The clerk seemed happy to see someone in the store and had brought out the phone book from a back room. She had no doubt that she could find someone in the development to direct her to the Prestons' street.

She'd like to ask Jerry about his late nights at Zig-Zag, especially Monday and even Friday when Denise was killed.

Wait a minute, Betty said to herself. You're not Jerry Preston's boss. He doesn't report to you.

The highway ran straight and true about a mile away from Hammond Center. Once on the highway she could easily find the exit to the new residential development that had been designed for prosperous young couples. She'd driven along the carefully laid out streets once with her realtor but had instantly known that a community with that many bicycles and tricycles in the front yards of extravagantly large, brand-new houses was not for her.

As she drove toward her paycheck, she wondered if it had been determined that Amanda Glyn had died around the time Jerry had logged off the computer in the programmers' room. In that event, he was undoubtedly under close scrutiny by the police. If it was later, it could be argued that a reputed computer genius with wicked intentions could surely have fiddled with the computer to make it look like he'd logged off at any time he chose.

It continued to seem highly unlikely that Amanda would be hanging about at three or four in the morning. She had been dressed for the funeral. Betty was hard-pressed to imagine her getting up at one or two, dressing in her little blue suit, and going off to Zig-Zag in her sneakers. A time closer to dawn seemed more logical. She supposed that Jerry could have logged off and then waited for Amanda, but that scenario didn't fit Betty's idea of the murder. And surely Nicole would have known if he'd been out all night and mentioned it when she'd stormed in. Or would she?

Betty passed a green and white highway sign indicating that the exit to Hodders Woods was a half mile ahead.

Everything looked clean and new at the bottom of the exit ramp: new gas stations, a row of new stores, two new stone pillars at the entrance to Hodders Woods. Betty viewed the big houses with a critical eye, now that she was a late-blooming homeowner herself. She wondered what sort of mortgages they carried, how much it cost to heat them, who would shovel the long driveways come the snows of winter.

A young mother pushing a stroller was the only person on the street. Betty drew up beside her and lowered her car window. "Hello, good morning. I'm trying to find Oriole Crescent."

The woman looked briefly alarmed at being accosted in her home territory but relaxed at the sight of a conventionally dressed older lady at the wheel of a sensible gray car. She and her bundled-up infant were not threatened by a potential murder/rapist/robber invading her safe bastion.

"Oh, gee. Sure. Let me see if I can tell you the way. I know it blindfolded, but when you try to tell somebody . . ." She closed her eyes—simulating the blindfold, perhaps. Betty got out her pocket notebook. "Take the second—no, the third right. First left on to Mockingbird until it ends. Right again on to Bluebird, and Oriole is the first left. There are only three houses. Who are you looking for?"

"The Prestons."

The woman almost, but not quite, rolled her eyes. "It's the big white house with the lovely Williamsburg blue trim. But Nicole has already hired a nanny for the little girl." There was a touch of envy in her voice and then a bit of sarcasm. "So she can run around as she chooses and play tennis at the club as early or late as she wants."

"I'm not applying for the job," Betty said. "I have business with Mr. Preston."

"I hope you're not a reporter or something," the young mother said. "The neighborhood is really bothered by all this police stuff and the murders. Poor Jerry. He's such a nice guy. It's been terrible for him and the little girl." She didn't mention poor Nicole.

"I work at his company," Betty said. "I had no idea he lived in a lovely community like this, where everybody knows everybody."

The young woman said slowly, "We're very friendly." The emphasis seemed to suggest that the Prestons perhaps were not. The infant began to wave its arms as though to signal that the pause had been long enough. Betty drove on before the hand motions gave way to vocal displeasure.

Betty found Oriole Crescent easily, a circular road with no other outlet. The three houses were widely spaced, with young trees planted between them, the beginning of protective barriers to maintain privacy. Older trees, no doubt the remnants of the original Hodders Woods, were visible behind the houses. Betty imagined swimming pools and elaborate barbecues out back and lawn chairs shaded by umbrellas.

There were two cars in the Prestons' driveway, very nice ones. One of them looked like the car Nicole had been driving the day of the funeral.

When she rang the doorbell, a buxom young woman with a circle of blond braids on the top of her head answered.

"We do not buy from the door, yes?" She had a faint Scandinavian or German accent.

"I'm looking for Mr. Preston. Elizabeth Trenka."

"Who is it, Ingrid?" a woman's voice called out from a room off the entrance hall.

"A lady for Mr. Preston."

Nicole was quickly out of the room into the hall, ready to chase her away. "He's not at home. Oh, it's you." She was wearing a white tennis outfit, complete with colorful sweatbands on her wrists and a sweater around her shoulders with the arms loosely knotted at her collarbone. She looked as though she hadn't slept well. "What do you want? Zig-Zag is closed and everything is being handled by my father."

"Your father suggested I come around."

Nicole looked astonished. "Whatever for?"

"My pay," Betty said. "I'm a temp, not on the company payroll."

"Oh, really! Everyone wants money from us." Nicole rounded on the girl, who had been attending to the exchange with interest. "Go along, Ingrid. You know what you're supposed to do. Finish up in the kitchen and then iron the clothes when the dryer is finished. And *please* be careful with my things."

"Yes, ma'am," the girl said, "but—"

"Don't argue. If you have any questions, I'll be finished here shortly."

The Prestons' new nanny bobbed her head humbly. Betty thought this was an example of poor management, and never mind that the girl had come from abroad to mind the Prestons' child and was now being kept busy by Nicole doing the housekeeping chores.

"Jerry is not available," Nicole said. "I'll tell him to send you the money you want so badly. Give me your address."

"I really have to see him," Betty said. "I have some other matters to discuss." She again tried her firm tone that indicated she wasn't brooking any nonsense.

But neither was Nicole Preston. "Absolutely not. I'd like to know what the likes of you needs to discuss with my husband."

Betty decided to be immovable. Before she would even consider mentioning her suspicions, even to Ted Kelso, she wanted to try to determine whether Jerry or anyone else, including Amanda, had known of Denise's relationship with Mr. Mitsui.

"It's about the murders," she said.

"He knows nothing about them. What business is it of yours?"

"The police have told me . . ." Betty began. "It's rather important." It was a calculated move to provide a tantalizing hint, to see if Nicole would summon Jerry. Or perhaps if he was listening from the other room . . .

"I said he wasn't here," Nicole said. She was breathing heavily, as though attempting to suppress her agitation. "Give me your address. He's out running. I don't know when he'll be back."

Given that the two cars were outside, Betty was inclined to believe her. "I will leave my address and telephone number. Please have him call me as soon as possible."

"I do not take orders from the help," Nicole said. "Especially women who don't know enough to keep their mouths shut when the police ask questions about me."

"They asked no questions," Betty said. "I simply told them you'd been there. I had no choice."

"My father," she began, then tilted her head and examined Betty more closely. "How is it you spoke to my father today?"

"Mr. Hammond arrived at Zig-Zag this morning while I was there."

"We closed it. They were there half the night. What were you doing there?"

"I went to work. No one told me the place was closed, and as long as I was there, I felt the need to look at the office where poor Amanda Glyn was murdered. Since I found her, I thought I'd confirm my impressions of the scene."

"And did you? Surely you didn't reach a conclusion when the police haven't."

"Oh, yes," Betty said. "I have a good idea what happened, but I don't care to say anything yet. I have to discuss the matter with Mr. Mitsui when we dine this evening."

"How do you know *him*?" Nicole sounded more agitated.

"He was connected with Denise and Zig-Zag, as you know," Betty said. "So naturally . . . Good day, Mrs. Preston."

Betty knew Nicole was watching her from the door as she got into her car, but she didn't look back.

CHAPTER 18

BETTY WAS slightly more cheerful about her second retirement than her first, but she was not happy about the sudden closing of Zig-Zag. Unless she involved herself with Mr. Mitsui, she'd never know the whys of the murders.

Ted Kelso had said that he was to be at Denise's house today, so she decided to return home by way of Prospect Street, in case he was already there sifting through her possessions. It would be hard for him to be reminded of the woman he'd cared about in ways Betty wasn't prepared to examine. Her recent news of Zig-Zag might divert him. Her conclusions, she decided, would remain hers for the present.

She imagined Alan Brown in his house up on the hill looking through the trees at the home of the woman he might have married. Or would he have? She was certain now that he would steadfastly deny their relationship now that Denise was dead.

She was thinking so hard at the traffic light in East Moulton that the car behind her blew its horn insistently when she failed to notice the light had changed to green.

She knew how Denise had found Zig-Zag, but how had she found Mr. Mitsui and what would her reward have been if Mr. Mitsui's organization acquired Zig-Zag and all its software? Perhaps the same reward would be dangled in front of Betty this evening.

The country road wound its way past scattered houses. It was much like her own Timberhill Road: a few new homes and a number of old-fashioned places. One or two looked as though they might once have been farmhouses like Eve's.

She wondered where Eve was now—traveling across the flat fields of Kansas or somewhere close by, in New York City perhaps, ensnared by the false promises of its neon lights. Betty passed Eve's house but did not stop at the produce stand, which today was loaded with pumpkins; half-gallons of cider; baskets of tomatoes, squash, and apples; trays of carrots and onions; and a heap of green and purple cabbages. An unfamiliar man was sitting in a wooden chair leaning back against the side of the stand. He looked young enough to be one of Eve's brothers.

She turned into the drive that led up to Denise's house.

There was no car about to indicate that Ted Kelso had arrived. She noted that there was a ramp with a gentle incline beside the steps to the landing outside Denise's back door where the driveway ended. Denise had been thoughtful enough to make it possible for her friend Ted Kelso to visit.

It seemed pointless to get out of the car, but as she looked at the door it appeared to be slightly ajar. She hesitated. It was entirely possible that someone had driven Ted here and left him to inventory and sort Denise's belongings.

The doorbell chimed loudly when she pushed the button, but no one responded. Since the door was already open a few inches, she pushed it wider with her toe.

"Ah!" She spoke aloud involuntarily.

The kitchen before her was in a shambles—drawers open, cupboard doors flung wide, jars and cans with their contents spilled onto the counters and floor. Her first thought was that the publicized death of Denise Legrand had aroused the larcenous instincts of someone in her quiet little town. When could this have happened? Had anyone noticed strangers on the street?

She walked warily through the kitchen along a short hallway into a spacious dining room. On the other side of the foyer through an archway she could see a large living room tastefully decorated in pastels, with subdued prints on some of the furniture. The rampage had continued into the dining room with the glasses from the breakfront swept from the shelves, leaving shards of crystal splattered across the beige rug. In the living room books from the bookcases were strewn across the floor, cushions from the sofas and chairs had been tossed about.

Betty listened. Not a sound anywhere in the house.

I should be alarmed, she thought, but it's so quiet. She couldn't determine whether it was simple vandalism or whether someone had been searching the house.

She started into the living room and stopped short. A denim jacket with a pattern of silver studs on the front had been tossed on a chair.

Eve? Betty couldn't believe that Eve had done this furious damage, but here was a sign that she'd been there. It appeared that she'd not run away from East Moulton but had sought refuge from her fears in the dead woman's house.

The idea of blackmail came back. If Eve had thought that what she had seen when Denise died would bring her the money she needed to leave East Moulton, what better place to hide than here and summon the person who would pay for her silence?

Silence. The house was so silent. Suddenly Betty did become alarmed. She didn't want to be here alone. In the kitchen, near a door for a quick exit, she used the wall phone to dial information and then Ted Kelso.

"I'm at Denise's house," she said. "I hoped to find you here, but now I've found ... Please change your plans. Come at once. I'll wait until you come before I call the police."

Fortunately, Ted didn't argue, didn't even ask many questions. He simply said, "Are you all right? Good. It takes me a little time to load the wheelchair into the car. Have you found another body?"

"Not yet," Betty said, "but I haven't really looked."

She wondered then if she should look—out in the sunroom, upstairs in the bedrooms. What if Eve had surprised

Denise's and Amanda's murderer, or had she telephoned the person she'd seen that night by the bridge? If the murderer had chosen to solve the problem of blackmail with another murder, Eve might be lying somewhere in this house. She might even still be clinging to her young life.

Betty felt she had a duty to investigate after all. It seemed unlikely that the murderer was in the house, but she considered carrying a carving knife or a poker from the fireplace. Then she realized that they were poor defenses. This killer resorted to bashing unsuspecting victims. Betty at least would not be caught by surprise.

The stairs brought her to a hallway with two bedrooms and a kind of study–television room opening off it. The ransacker had been up here, too, but there was no sign of Eve—except for a bed that appeared to have been slept in. In the television room she found a couple of empty diet Coke cans and a *TV Guide* open to Tuesday evening. That seemed to indicate that Eve had been here last night. What could have happened? She'd either been kidnapped, leaving her jacket behind, or she'd run out into the night. Betty shivered. Her car seemed like the best place to wait for Ted, away from this mess.

It wasn't long before his car came up the driveway.

"Can I help you?" she asked as Ted opened the car door.

He grinned at her from the driver's seat and reached around to the wheelchair that was stowed behind the backseat. "No help necessary," he said. "I managed to arrange my life so that retired ladies of firm convictions and a doubtful circle of acquaintances, including a murderer, would not be required to assist." He maneuvered the wheelchair out of the car, unfolded it, and eased himself into it. "Let's go. It was good of Denise to have the ramp put in. Now start explaining."

She told him how she'd gotten in and what she'd found. "I recognized Eve's jacket. She must have been hiding here for a couple of days. She's gone. I looked upstairs to be sure—"

"She wasn't dead," he finished for her. "Foolhardy but honorable."

"This is turning out to be the most dangerous part of Connecticut I've ever spent time in," Betty said.

"Did you touch anything?"

"Only the kitchen phone to call you."

"We have to tell the police," he said as he surveyed the destruction. "Although our reputations with them are becoming tarnished at an unprecedented rate." He moved through the dining room into the living room. "Denise didn't keep anything important here. She had a computer upstairs with which she used to send me Prodigy messages. It was hooked up to the office by modem so she could communicate from home. She didn't have information anyone would want this badly."

"Do we assume that the intruder was her murderer searching for something?" Betty asked.

"Ninety-percent sure, wouldn't you say? Look at this place. Robbers like to empty out drawers and take away the odd valuable bits everybody has, but this looks as though someone was looking for something hidden behind books, hidden in the kitchen."

"Not a document. Mr. Mitsui said there was no proof of their arrangement. But what about Jerry's new software? Denise gave you a copy," Betty said. "Maybe she had another here and somebody wanted it. Anyhow, it happened last night." She explained about the *TV Guide*. Then she explained her idea about blackmail. "If Eve escaped, the murderer is still in the same dangerous position as ever."

"If I hadn't begun to trust your judgment," Ted said, "I would now be thinking you'd gone over into fantasy."

"I don't want to tell anyone about my ideas yet," Betty said. "But bad news for Jerry Preston—he was working into the small hours on Monday night at Zig-Zag. The police must be circling around him for Amanda's death at least." She shook her head. "It's impossible, though. I think you ought to call the police."

"Me?"

"You've lived in this town for a while without noticeable recourse to homicide, or Penny Saks would surely have told me. I'm an unknown quantity, and besides, our state trooper is, to quote him, very, very disappointed in me."

"What now?"

"I didn't tell you the other night, but I willfully distorted the truth about Mr. Mitsui at Zig-Zag. I suppose I thought I was being protective of the company. Old habits die hard. And I really didn't think Mr. Mitsui had murdered Amanda Glyn in between telephone calls to Tokyo, so I didn't mention he'd found Amanda first. The trooper found out later. I'm rather ashamed."

"Elizabeth, you have nothing to be ashamed of."

Ted made the call.

"We're to stay put, touching nothing, until someone comes. Now you can tell me what's been going on. Why aren't you at Zig-Zag?"

"Closed until further notice, just like that. Jerry is escaping from his problems by running. George Hammond is now Mr. Mitsui's great friend, if the old arm around the shoulders means anything. Mr. Mitsui is now my great friend as well. No," she said with a smile, "he's not my friend. He's my date. We're dining tonight."

"Is he toying with your affections," Ted asked, "or are his intentions honorable?"

"I'm sure Mr. Mitsui is entirely honorable in his own eyes. Anyhow, you told me to find out what he wants from me."

"You can ask him tonight."

"I intend to, although I won't be surprised if he doesn't tell me plainly. Mr. Mitsui is not forthcoming unless it suits him." She looked around the devastated room. "I'd like to know what he promised Denise so she felt she could announce these so-called marriage plans."

"What does that mean?" Ted leaned forward on the arm of his wheelchair and looked at her intently.

"I saw Alan Brown this morning. They certainly had been meeting privately. In fact, Amanda Glyn hinted to me that she'd seen Denise out with a boyfriend. However, he denied absolutely that they were planning to marry. He said Denise might have gotten some mistaken idea . . ."

Ted seemed to relax.

"He probably saw it as a way to escape his mother, and then when Denise died he chose not to disturb the home front."

"Does Mrs. Brown wield so much power?"

"Denise never talked about Alan. I don't know. It may all have come down to money. If Denise made a lot from the Mitsui deal, he wouldn't have had to worry about his mother holding on to the bank books. His father left a sizable estate, according to town gossip."

"I feel that he didn't kill her," Betty said, "without any proof. He did arrange for Denise to work at Zig-Zag, though, via Nicole, whom I also spoke to this morning. I visited the Preston house. Very grand, complete with a new European nanny named Ingrid. Nicole wasn't very welcoming."

"I suppose she wouldn't be," Ted said, "if her husband is under suspicion of murder. Could Jerry have done this?" He waved at the destruction around them.

Betty shook her head. "There's no doubt he's under suspicion. He doesn't seem the type to solve problems with murder. But at least the police may start looking for Eve seriously now, and here they come."

The man and the woman who came in were unknown to Betty, but the shoulder patches on their uniforms indicated they were local East Moulton police.

Ted explained. Betty explained. They looked about. Betty explained some more, this time about Eve.

"The state trooper is coming. Did anybody touch anything?"

Betty confessed to using the phone and looking about briefly.

"I'm supposed to be inventorying the house," Ted said. "I'm Miss Legrand's executor. I'll do it later, of course."

"We'll just be in the way if we stay around," Betty said, and edged toward the door.

"They'll want to talk to you," the officer said.

"They know where to find me," Ted said. "I'm not feeling at all well, Elizabeth. I wonder if you could help me home, if the officers don't object."

Both officers glanced at the wheelchair. "Sure. Okay. We understand," the woman officer said.

Outside Betty said, "You're not being truthful about not feeling well."

He looked sideways at her as he opened his car door and prepared to shift from the wheelchair to the driver's seat. "I feel fine. I couldn't think of a better way to avoid a long wait and stupid questions we had no answers for."

"Devious," she said.

"Come along to my place," he said. "I want to talk more about what you did today."

"I did a number of things before the day was barely begun," Betty said. "I think I know who the murderer is, but I can't be sure, and now I am very annoyed besides."

"Annoyed? Is that the correct reaction?"

"It is terrible that two people are dead, and poor Eve has been terrorized. I'd like to see justice done, but Zig-Zag has been closed, probably for good. Those poor girls are out of work. Marsha's husband likely won't want her to go to work elsewhere; Eileen won't be able to save up for her wedding. The economy isn't good. Will Tanya find another job easily? Reuben? Mr. Caruso isn't all that young. It will be hard for him. The programmers love their work and that's been taken from them. 'Not fair,' one of them told me. Absolutely right. I understand what it's like to be pushed out. It's thoughtless, selfish, and morally indefensible."

"Ah, that anger is still there, Elizabeth. Think about what you have—"

"What I have is a good idea of who must have done it and the feeling that I should help see that justice is done."

"And how will you accomplish that?"

"I'm not sure," Betty said, "but I've never liked to see business left unfinished."

CHAPTER 19

"You look thoughtful," Ted said as he poured Betty some excellent coffee he'd made from freshly ground beans. It was several miles ahead of Betty's instant.

"It's because I'm thinking," she said. She carried her coffee mug around Ted's living space, pausing to look at the titles of books, movies on tape and laser disc, and compact discs that covered centuries of music: symphonies, concertos, chamber music, opera, old-time rock 'n' roll (Elvis did live, here), country and western, and the latest in current popular music. She knew some of the names but doubted that she would recognize the music. Rap, she had decided sometime before, was not designed to appeal to her age group.

"If Jerry Preston is guilty of something," Ted said, "a lot of people will go out of their way to cover for him."

"Like his wife, you mean?" Betty said. "She would know if he was out on the nights of both murders, although she could lie about that to the authorities. Indeed, she seems capable of lying about anything to protect her territory. In any case, Jerry can claim that he was working on some computer program in the basement of Zig-Zag. The computers will show him logging in and out."

She walked to the windows that looked out on the garden at the back of the house. She could see what she supposed were Ted's beehives in a row at the end of the property.

"Jerry knows he's under suspicion. I know he was out somewhere on one and perhaps both nights in question, so the police must know, too. They're probably also trying to determine the whereabouts of George Hammond. He'd been out in California but had returned apparently by Friday at the latest. George said that Denise had told him about Mr. Mitsui arriving unexpectedly in the United States. Maybe that was one of the calls she told you she had to make after your dinner. The police are also probably checking up on Mr. Mitsui—they went as far as to confirm that he was at the Waldorf in New York on Friday night. The girls at the office didn't care for either Denise or Amanda, but none of them appears to possess the kind of passionate hatred that would seem to be required.

"Finally, they've spoken to Alan Brown—naturally, since he found Denise's body. They talked to all of the neighbors, he said. No one saw anything. Except perhaps Eve."

"I wonder if anyone saw anything last night," Ted said. "More coffee?"

"Thanks," Betty said, and filled her mug. "A car, maybe. Or lights in the house while Eve was there, although the blinds were all down. Ted, there's a good chance that she was thinking of blackmail. Who was it who said that blackmail is a childish way to make some money?"

"You know what I meant."

"Well, here we have a child who probably thinks she invented the idea."

Ted moved his wheelchair away from her to his computer. "I put down all the things we talked about last night." He tapped out some numbers, then watched the figures and words rearrange themselves on the screen. "When I run the facts through this little spreadsheet program to see who matches up with what, I don't come up with anything significant."

"It's too logical," Betty said. "It needs intuition, and so few computers I've encountered have a program for that."

"Don't talk like a technophobe," he said impatiently.

"I'm not. I'm saying that close to forty years of working with people in offices—just being alive for sixty-three years—gives you a good deal of experience in sensing what's going on beneath the surface, behind the facts. I said

I was annoyed about Zig-Zag, but what I am is angry—and not," she added, "because I didn't get paid. Murder is a bad management practice. I was in Denise's office early this morning, imagining the scene: Amanda behind the desk, the murderer standing beside her." Ted listened carefully as she explained what she had imagined the scene had been like and why. "A presumption of equality. It applies somewhat to Denise's death, too," she said finally.

Ted said slowly, "You might well be correct in your assumptions. But intuition is not the kind of proof that's needed. I have an idea." The doorbell interrupted him. "That should be the police. We did run out on`them." He spoke through the intercom, then opened the door to their state trooper. "Well, Officer. Come in. Miss Trenka and I were discussing these terrible events."

Betty was mildly amused by Ted's hearty welcome. He sounded like the Edwards & Son controller who had been pretty sure he'd been discovered with his hand in the till but had decided to bluff it out, just in case. She remembered the sound of the fellow twenty years ago, when Sid Senior had called him into his office to discuss puzzling financial irregularities. Betty had been there at Sid's side.

"Let me get you some coffee," Ted said.

"No thanks," the trooper said. "Miss Trenka, we meet again." He looked at her. "And again and again."

"You're here because of the trouble at Denise's place," Ted said. "I'd say it was some local who heard about her death and decided to take a look around, mess things up a little. It didn't appear that anything had been taken."

"You know the house well?" the trooper asked.

"Well enough," Ted said. "Unless someone made off with her jewelry. Denise had some nice pieces that I understood she kept in her bedroom. I wasn't able to get upstairs."

"No. I mean, yes. I can see that. There wasn't any jewelry found, only a couple of empty cases in a drawer."

Betty looked at Ted quickly. Eve could have taken the pieces after failing to get a blackmail payoff.

"Did Miss Legrand keep anything else of value at her house? Documents, confidential material connected with the business?"

"Not that I know of." Ted didn't mention their speculation about the new software.

"About this Evelyn Cursey," the trooper said. "Her mother identified the jacket found in the house. The girl seems to have been hiding out there. She was probably there on Tuesday night."

"You noticed the *TV Guide*," Betty said.

The trooper frowned at her.

"I had to go upstairs to see if the poor girl was lying there murdered," Betty said defensively. "We were wondering if anyone had noticed anything during the night."

The trooper hesitated, then shrugged. "Nobody on Prospect Street saw anything unusual except for a car parked near the bridge for a short time. No license or model noted. You suggested the other day that Evelyn might have witnessed the crime against Miss Legrand." He looked at Betty.

"I thought she seemed frightened," Betty said. "The way she spoke of the murder . . ."

"Nothing more than that? Just what you thought?"

"I know," she said firmly. "I just don't know who or what she was frightened about, but look what's happened."

The trooper shook his head. "Not much to go on, ma'am. However, we are taking Evelyn's disappearance seriously, since she was at the house and there have been these two deaths."

"That's something," Betty said. "Officer—"

"Call me Bob," he said. "It will simplify things. Unless I arrest you. Then you can call me sir."

"Well, Bob," she began, but it didn't sound right. She decided she would avoid addressing him by name. "Mr. Kelso and I have a deep interest in this business. He was devoted to Miss Legrand. I worked at the company where both women were employed. We want to know who the police suspect and why."

Bob was a bit taken aback but seemed amused.

"I don't think I can tell you that," he said. "And we are not absolutely sure the two deaths are connected."

"Of course they are," she said impatiently. She was standing beside Ted's wheelchair facing the trooper. Two against one. "Why can't you tell us? Are we among the suspects?" She assumed her sternest expression that had successfully cowed office-supply salesmen, copier repairmen, and even the men from the telephone company.

"You are not suspects," Bob said, then added, "at this time. To tell the truth, we don't have many indications pointing toward a specific perpetrator. I wonder if either of you can tell me anything pertinent about Jerry Preston."

"What motive would he have? Give us a motive."

Bob briefly registered disbelief. "Ma'am, people don't usually demand information from me in quite that tone of voice."

"Now, Elizabeth," Ted said soothingly, "Bob is just doing his job, and it's our job to help him." He looked up at her sideways and winked almost imperceptibly.

"I apologize," Betty said. "It's been upsetting. And I feel responsible for Mr. Kelso's mental and emotional well-being at this very trying time." She had no doubt that Ted had firm control over both his mind and his emotions, but they all seemed to be swept up in an improvisation that had no apparent end in sight. "I shouldn't have been short with you."

She had the trooper a little off balance now. She knew when to toady as well as to command.

"About Jerry Preston . . ." Bob waited. "Look, we know he often works on his computer stuff at the company offices at night, but he claims to have gone home well before Miss Glyn was killed and wasn't out at all the night Miss Legrand died, according to him and his wife."

Betty frowned. Ted frowned. This was not true.

"What about the Japanese fellow?" Ted asked.

"He said he didn't know Miss Glyn."

"Do you know how Amanda got to Zig-Zag?"

"We found Miss Glyn's car in the Hammond Center mall parking lot. But no one can tell us how she got into the building."

"No problem getting in," Betty said. "She had Marsha's key."

"What?" Bob was distinctly startled.

"Didn't Marsha tell you? She's the blond girl who works in accounting at Zig-Zag. She probably forgot." Betty hated putting poor Marsha on the spot and perhaps giving her husband occasion to treat her unkindly. "After work on Monday Amanda borrowed the key Marsha was assigned for this week."

Betty realized as she said it that it suggested that Amanda was probably already planning to meet her murderer during the day on Monday. She didn't think, however, that the trooper would welcome further comments on the investigation from her.

Bob asked a few more questions about the break-in, but his heart didn't seem to be in it since neither Betty nor Ted had anything to add. Betty thought, as he left, that the state trooper uniform was rather handsome in an intimidating sort of way.

"We know Jerry is suspected," Ted said when they were alone. "We know that the Prestons probably didn't tell the complete truth about him being at home." He reached for the phone book, found a number, and dialed. "Mr. Preston, please. He's not? When will he be back? Is Mrs. Preston in, then? I see. No message." He grinned at Betty. "It will take you about twenty minutes to get over to Hodders Woods. Jerry won't be back until this evening, Nicole is playing tennis and lunching at the country club." He scratched his head. "The girl was rather talkative. Funny thing she said. Nicole is playing tennis with a Mr. Brown."

"Alan? Sharing his grief with a trusted old girlfriend? Doesn't he work?"

"Not much. He's a lawyer, but he doesn't practice. You'll have plenty of time in Hodders Woods without interference."

"Exactly what will I be doing in Hodders Woods?"

"Talking to that nanny. You'll ask what she knows about Jerry's comings and goings. I'm sure the police will talk to her eventually, if they haven't already, but I'll bet you can be nice and grandmotherly."

"Kindly, perhaps," Betty said. "Grandmotherly is beyond me. Still, she'd probably welcome kindness. She cooks, she cleans, she sweeps up the ashes like Cinderella. She's the built-in baby-sitter, new to the community and without a friend."

"Until you."

"For heaven's sake," Betty said, but she was thinking less about Ted's characterizations than about something she remembered about poor Eve, without a friend, now that Denise was gone. Then she said, "All right, I'll try. At least I know what I want to find out."

"That's only the first thing you have to do," Ted said. "Then I think you ought to drop by the country club. Have lunch."

"Me? I don't belong, and don't intend to."

"I know the man in charge," Ted said. "I'll fix it. The glassed-in terrace will be nice, in case it turns chilly."

CHAPTER 20

THE FOG with which the day had begun had burned off and the sun had broken through the remaining thin layer of clouds. Nicole Preston would be playing tennis with her old friend Alan in the autumn sun, while Ingrid pursued imaginary dustballs under the beds at the Preston home and scrubbed away invisible smudges from its clean, new walls.

Betty didn't pause at her house but drove along the back roads up to the highway. Ted had been right. It was only a bit more than twenty minutes until she reached Oriole Crescent. There were no cars in the driveway of the Preston house, but the door of the two-car garage attached to the split-level house was lowered. She hoped Nicole hadn't had a change of plans and come home early, putting her car away in the garage.

When she rang the doorbell, she could hear it sound faintly somewhere in the house, but no one answered the door. She rang it again, then glanced around. The neighborhood was quiet: no cars, no children at play, no mothers with strollers. There were no dandelions thrusting up through the perfect lawns, while bronze and yellow chrysanthemums bloomed peacefully in decorative pots and precise flowerbeds in front of the three houses on Oriole Crescent.

Betty left the front steps and crossed the grass to the side of the house. From there she could see a stretch of lawn sloping down to meet the old stand of woods. There was indeed a fenced-in swimming pool and two round white tables with blue-and-white-striped umbrellas in their centers.

A black Weber barbecue was surrounded by wooden lawn chairs with thick blue cushions. It was a choice spot. Unless a developer uprooted the woods, no one would build behind the Preston house.

Beyond the pool Ingrid was sitting on the grass while the Preston child, a little girl of four or five in jeans and a T-shirt, seemed to be acting out a story. Ingrid clapped her hands at the climax of the child's charade, and the little girl ran to her and hugged her around the neck.

Betty walked down the gentle incline toward them, past the pool and the barbecue.

The child noticed her first and let go of Ingrid. She stood watching Betty with her thumb in her mouth. Ingrid looked up quickly, then stood, placing herself in front of the child as Betty approached.

Betty waved reassuringly. "It's only me, Betty Trenka," she called out. "I was here this morning."

Ingrid waited. She had on a plain white blouse and a flower-print skirt and her blond braids were a pale halo in the weak midday sun.

"They are out of the house, yes?" Ingrid said when Betty was within a few feet of her. "Mr. Preston says he goes to the office. She is playing the tennis."

"I'll see them later," Betty said. "I wanted to speak to you."

"To speak to me?" Ingrid reached out and pulled the child closer to her. The child peered around Ingrid to watch Betty.

"I have been worried . . ."

"But I am well," Ingrid said. "Kathy is well."

"Worried about Mr. and Mrs. Preston, I meant. The pressure from these murders. Have the police spoken to you?"

Ingrid looked wary. "I speak . . . I have spoken with a man from the police, but Mrs. Preston is with me when they come. They ask if I ever see these ladies who are dead, but I do not know them. I do not know anyone here but Mr. and Mrs. Preston and the little girl's grandpa, who comes here."

"Grandpa," the child said.

"On Monday night, did the Prestons go out?"

"Monday? I think it is like every night. After Kathy and I eat, we watch a video of Raffi, the singer for children, yes? I bathe Kathy and she is put into bed. I watch television in the room where I sleep next to the nursery, then I sleep. Before I hear Mr. and Mrs. Preston speaking in the living room."

"So you didn't hear or see either of them leave?"

Ingrid appeared to be considering this. "I am a stranger here. I do not understand these matters. I care for the little girl. That is my job, not what the father and mother do." She was uneasy, no question about it.

But Betty was persistent. "They both left, then," she said, and Ingrid did not deny it. "At what hour did they return here?"

"I am asleep," Ingrid said vehemently. "I do not know. I do not know anything about this. Please leave. Mrs. Preston will not be happy to find you here."

"Oh, but she's not home."

Ingrid gave up. "The child will tell her and she will be angry with me. This one talks all the time when there are no strangers."

Betty bent down to the little girl, who stared at her mute and round-eyed. "What a pretty little girl you are," she said. "Are you happy to have your new friend Ingrid here?"

The child nodded tentatively.

"Do you like her as much as your friend Evelyn? Eve?"

The child half nodded and shrugged at the same time. Ingrid tightened her protective arm around the child.

"This girl you speak of, Evelyn. The little girl liked her. She was here on Monday in the afternoon, but Mrs. Preston sent her away. She said that it would upset the child to see her. I think this is foolish. It was this Evelyn who was upset."

"I see," Betty said. "And yesterday, Tuesday. Mr. and Mrs. Preston went away early?"

"Mr. Preston was not here when I went to the kitchen at

eight as I am required to do to make the little girl's breakfast. Mrs. Preston is still asleep, I think, but the telephone rings and it must be she who answers. She does not come to the kitchen to see the little girl but drives away in the car. It is confusing to me. I have worked for some very fine families, but with . . . mmm . . . regular habits, yes?"

"I'm sure things will settle down," Betty said. "If you find that you are having problems, please telephone me and I will try to help." She scribbled her telephone number on a page from her notebook. "I don't want you to feel that you are all alone in a strange country."

Ingrid looked at her for a long minute, then took the slip of paper and put it in her pocket.

Betty started to walk back up the gentle incline toward the front of the house. Halfway there she looked up at the house but immediately continued on her way. She was certain she had seen a figure standing at one of the upper windows looking down on the backyard. She couldn't tell if it was a man or a woman, but she knew she didn't want to come face-to-face with either Jerry or Nicole.

As she rounded the corner of the house, she stopped. A car was parked in the driveway. It did not appear to be either of the two she had seen there earlier. She looked around, but no one was in sight on the sidewalks of Oriole Crescent. She had her car keys in her hand and hoped she could speed away before the person came out from the house.

Her hand was on the car when she heard a familiar voice bellowing from the open front door of the Preston house.

"You there! Stop where you are!"

Betty stopped. George Hammond didn't scare her, but he was among the people she didn't care to meet just now. He was coming down the walk toward her. She wondered if he could possibly be holding his breath to make his face get redder and redder as he approached. She decided it was pure annoyance at the sight of her.

"Mr. Hammond," Betty said, "what a surprise to see you here."

"You're the surprise," he said. "This is my daughter's house, I have every reason to be here. What I want to know is what you thought you're doing talking to that girl."

"I was looking for Mr. and Mrs. Preston. I must say your granddaughter is a lovely child." He seemed like the kind of man who would soften under sentimental comments about an angelic-looking grandchild. He was.

"She's a real sweetheart, loves her grandpa," he said. Then he scowled. "What did you want to see them about? Are you still looking to get paid?" He gazed at her speculatively, as though wondering why a friend of Mr. Mitsui's was so eager for her few dollars. He didn't wait for her answer. "Jerry's out and so is Nicole."

"I know. She's playing tennis."

"She's the kind who'd keep batting those balls around if the world were coming to an end." He seemed almost proud of the idea.

Betty said, "What I really want is a clearer idea of the status of Zig-Zag. The girls at the office need to know."

"Them." Hammond's tone dismissed the staff's problems.

"And I need to know precisely what is going on with Zig-Zag if I am to be of any help."

"This is not any business of yours."

"It *is* a question of two murders," Betty said, "and I did find one body. I intend to go around to Zig-Zag this afternoon to discuss the matter with Jerry."

"That idiot. Can't explain himself to the police, off on a cloud with his computers, paying no attention to my little girl. I give him a business to run and he's set on making a lousy deal with Mitsui. The man's too smart for him, but I'll straighten things out. I can handle anything." That vein in his temple was throbbing again. He was not good at dealing with stress.

"I understood that Denise Legrand was handling things perfectly. Do you suppose that's why she was killed?"

He looked at her coldly. "I wouldn't be surprised, but I'll

tell you this. My little girl has better business sense than that woman ever did. It runs in the family."

Betty thought that poor management techniques were the thing she noticed running in the Hammond family.

"Yet she didn't choose to work for Zig-Zag?" she asked.

"Too many other important responsibilities," he said shortly. "Mitsui seems to think highly of you." He eyed her suspiciously. "You one of his flunkies?"

Betty thought for a moment. The truth wasn't especially distinguished. Then suddenly she felt empowered. It didn't matter what she said, especially since she had told Ted Kelso she wanted to see justice done.

"Mr. Mitsui is a fine man," she said. "We don't have too many opportunities to meet, what with him at one end of the world and me at the other."

"Well, Miss . . . ah . . . ?"

"Trenka," Betty said. "Elizabeth Trenka. I was formerly senior vice president at Edwards & Son. Do you know them?" Thankfully, Hammond shook his head. "They're up near Hartford. I handled the international side for years."

Remarkably, George Hammond did not blink at that tall story. The truth was, the modest bits of hardware that Edwards & Son manufactured did not lend themselves to either international business or commercial fame, but Betty had heard enough senior vice presidents through the years to be able to imitate one.

"So you knew Mitsui from before."

"From before this morning? Certainly. We've had some rather delicate dealings over time." Well, two days was a space of time, and one murder victim, one white lie to the police, and a doubtful offer to be taken on as Mr. Mitsui's spy could be construed as matters of delicacy. "I suppose you knew all about Denise Legrand's dealings with him," Betty said.

"That woman. She was up to something, all right. At least that's finished. Originally Mitsui wanted to take a couple of the buildings in the office park off my hands. Next thing I know, he's talking rights to some of Zig-Zag software, and then it's this new stuff Jerry dreamed up that I don't understand. Not even on the market yet. He moved right in on us, and I know Denise was behind it."

"She was," Betty said. "Confidentially, I believe she had a private arrangement with Mr. Mitsui."

"Is that a fact," Hammond said. "Well, she doesn't anymore, does she?"

"And Amanda Glyn won't have a chance to take her place at Jerry's side."

"That tramp," Hammond said. Then he tilted his head and looked at her. "When I saw you in the office a couple of days ago, didn't you say you were a temp?"

"Temporary consulting assignment," Betty said quickly. "Ah, yes. I was answering the phones. Such fun. I haven't done that in years, but when I saw how upset things were, I decided to pitch in and help."

"I wonder if you and I could come to some arrangement," Hammond said. "I might be able to use you. I'll need someone at Zig-Zag after this trouble blows over."

Betty admired his optimism about the happy outcome of fairly significant "trouble." She didn't want to cut herself off from the connection with Zig-Zag by an outright refusal, but she certainly didn't want to find herself acting as Hammond's negotiating agent while she was being offered the same role by Mr. Mitsui. A dramatic upward career move, she thought wryly, for the former office manager of Edwards & Son.

"Could we discuss this at a later time?" she asked. "I have an urgent appointment right now."

"I've got a cellular phone," he said. He handed her a business card. "Call me and I'll get back to you. You know, Nicole told me not to trust Denise."

"And Amanda?"

He almost rolled his eyes. "That one was trouble."

"Yes. I heard the usual office gossip about her." She went on quickly as Hammond glared at her, "Everyone hopes that the police will turn up the murderer soon to get Jerry off the hook."

"People who are members of my family are not on anybody's hook." Hammond marched toward the front door.

As she drove away from Oriole Crescent, she again considered the employment possibilities that had suddenly opened up for her: She could be Mr. Mitsui's agent or George Hammond's.

She wondered what the going rate was and whether they would offer to pay her up front or out of the profits.

CHAPTER 21

TED HAD described the route to the country club near Hodders Woods. "It's really quite modest," he'd told her, "but they've made it exclusive enough for people to want to belong. Of course, it was Hammond land that was sold to the company who developed the club, so Nicole and Jerry are probably life members without payment of dues."

Betty found the road to the country club and drove past rolling fairways and manicured greens. A few golfers were visible, mostly women, making their way from hole to hole in slick little golf carts. Their hardworking husbands would be out in force once the week ended.

The white clubhouse had a glassed-in terrace visible from the parking lot. Tennis courts were laid out at one side, but no one was playing. Again, the men were at work and the children had already started school. Nicole Preston and her partner Alan Brown had probably finished their game and gone to lunch.

The man who met her at the door of the dining room assured her that Ted Kelso had called and then led her out to a table on the terrace.

"Is Mrs. Preston here?" Betty asked. The room was nearly empty.

"She was, but she left a while ago after receiving a phone call." He pointed to a man sitting alone facing the windows and a view of the first tee. "Her tennis partner is still here." He leaned toward Betty and whispered, "Alan Brown."

"I know him," Betty said. "Perhaps you'd ask him if

he'd join me for lunch. Tell him Elizabeth Trenka from East Moulton."

"Of course."

"But," Betty added, "don't be troubled if he turns me down."

Alan Brown turned around when the man spoke in his ear. He stood up, looking fit in his white tennis shorts and shirt. After a moment's hesitation, he walked over to Betty's table.

"I don't know why you are hounding me," Alan said.

"I certainly am not," Betty said. "I was looking for Nicole Preston and was told she'd left. I saw that you were alone. Sit down, please, even if you don't care to have lunch."

He sat reluctantly.

"You may not have heard that someone vandalized Denise's house last night," she said.

Alan looked surprised. "I did think I saw a light the other night, but my mother told me I was dreaming."

"It was probably Eve," Betty said. "She was hiding out there and now she's run away again, probably from the person who wrecked the place."

He frowned. "Eve? Evelyn?"

"I'm convinced she knows who murdered Denise," she said. "Don't you want to know, too?"

"I want to know," he said softly.

"Do you have suspicions?"

"Yes," he said. "I'm sorry, I can't remember your name."

"Elizabeth Trenka." She waited. It was quiet and gracious here, with the green carpeting and white wicker chairs set around the tables, and warm enough even though some of the wide windows were open. Outside, some tennis players had taken over two of the courts and were practicing serves and volleys. Far in the distance a tiny golf cart headed toward a green surrounded by tall trees. Such a good life.

"Miss Trenka, I haven't been myself since Denise died. She did call me on my private line the night she was murdered. I was at home with my mother. She told me that everything would be settled after her trip to New York. She talked about marriage, how that would make everything perfect. I didn't argue with her, so maybe she got the idea . . . I should never have gotten her involved with the Prestons and their business. She was headstrong, thought she knew better than anyone else. She had some run-ins with Nicole and George Hammond, but Jerry smoothed it over. He's an okay guy. I did care about her, and I didn't kill her."

"Or Amanda Glyn?"

"I never laid eyes on her," Alan Brown said.

"Denise had known Mr. Mitsui for some time." It was less a question than a statement.

He nodded. "From back when Japanese businessmen first started coming to New York in numbers. The company she was with did business with his over the years."

"Did she say anything else when she called you? Anything that might indicate . . ." Betty supposed it was painful for Alan to talk about the death of his dream.

"Nothing much. She said she had to call George Hammond to warn him that Mitsui was in the States. She didn't want him to know that she was dealing behind his back, but of course she was. She said . . ." He stopped. "She said if everything worked, she'd end up taking over the company with Mitsui's backing. The Hammonds and the Prestons would be out and she'd be in."

"Otherwise, *sayonara*," she murmured.

"What?"

"Something I heard," Betty said. "No," she said to the waiter who had finally made his way to the table. "I've decided I don't care for lunch after all. Mr. Brown, do you know who called Nicole away?"

"Just a call for her was all the captain said. I thought it must be about Kathy the way she flew out of here."

"May I ask why you decided to play tennis with her today?"

"She decided. Begged me. And then all she could talk

about was how Jerry had messed everything up. She's not easy, you know. Years ago my mother thought we were the perfect couple. Couldn't have been more wrong." He gazed off across the golf course. "Nothing perfect about Nicole." He stood up. "I hope they discover who killed Denise soon. Good-bye, Miss Trenka."

She wondered who had called Nicole. Certainly not Ingrid, or Betty would have met her on the doorstep as she was leaving. Eve? Her father?

Betty thought she might be too old for this kind of business. She felt very sad about Jerry Preston. He seemed to be caught up in matters over which he had no control.

When she finally reached the little house that was now her home, it seemed especially welcoming.

The house was stuffy, since she'd left all the windows closed when she'd gone out so long ago in the early-morning fog. She wanted to rest but decided she ought to go across and speak with Ted about her visit to the Preston house and the country club.

First she'd relax for half an hour and read the *Ledger*, which was on the coffee table in her living room.

Betty stopped midway across the room.

The *Ledger* should be on her front doorstep, not in her living room.

"Hello?" she called. Had Mr. Mitsui come visiting again? These uninvited visitors were rather more than she'd bargained for. She went to the kitchen. She found no one there, but on the counter were the wrappings of two of her frozen dinners. Someone had heated them up and eaten them.

She felt like one of the three bears and wondered if she'd find Goldilocks asleep in her bed.

Betty went upstairs cautiously. The creak of the fourth step sounded loud enough to alert anyone above. She was certain she'd find Eve there, hiding out in the one place probably no one would think to look: the house of the new town resident.

Once again, however, Eve had departed.

Betty was relieved that, within the last few hours at least,

Eve had been alive and well, but where could she have gone now?

Downstairs, Betty picked up the phone to call Penny Saks. She hoped that the eyes of Timberhill Road had been fixed once again on Betty's house and that Penny had seen Eve come or go.

She almost missed seeing the note placed under the phone. In careful, almost childish writing it said: "I hope you don't mind I ate some stuff. I will pay you back when I have the money that I am going to get now in Hammond Center. I didn't hurt the back door, it was not hard to get in. Your friend, Eve Cursey."

"Penny? Betty Trenka. Did you notice a young girl leaving my house this afternoon? No, no. It was perfectly all right for her to be here. Yes, it was Eve. I'd forgotten she was your baby-sitter. I wondered what time she left." Betty listened as Penny talked. She could hear the voice of one Whitey or another in the background.

Eve had left about an hour ago, right after Ted Kelso had gone out. A car had driven up and she'd run out, gotten in, and been driven off in the direction of Main Street. Penny had thought it peculiar. No, it hadn't been the limousine. Just an ordinary car. She couldn't tell who was driving. She thought it might have been a boy, but she couldn't be sure.

What came to mind was the money Eve thought she was getting.

Blackmailers ran the great risk of never collecting, Betty thought. Then she thought she ought to do something about this.

Ted Kelso's phone responded with a taped message.

"I'm going to find Eve," Betty said to the answering machine. "I think she's gone to Zig-Zag. I'll call when I get back."

If I get back. The thought intruded briefly and was sent packing.

Don't be silly, she told herself. You haven't lived this long and gone through what you have to end up dead at the hands of a small-town murderer.

She took only a moment to change from her business clothes into a denim skirt and a lightweight black turtleneck. She slipped off her low-heeled office shoes and put on the ordinary blue tennis shoes she wore on weekends. No fancy high-tech running shoes for Betty Trenka. These were the old-fashioned sneakers she'd been buying for decades, although she remembered when canvas shoes like these had cost a mere five dollars or less. Those were the days.

As she stood at her front door, she tried to think of what she might need.

No weapon would defend her, except her wits.

A flashlight might come in handy, though. She had a little pocket one she always kept in a kitchen drawer in case she needed to seek out something in the back of a cabinet.

Once in her car, she knew she ought to hurry. Betty was most scrupulous about observing speed limits and traffic laws, but the more she thought about the possibility of Eve being at Zig-Zag alone with a dangerous person, the faster the speedometer edged up. She slowed a bit as she passed through the center of East Moulton. Molly Perkins was standing at the door of the drugstore, but Betty failed to respond to her wave. She'd hear about that, she didn't doubt. People were pumping their own gas at the service station, carrying clothes in plastic covers from the dry cleaners, coming and going at the library. The flag flew over the post office; the supermarket parking lot was full of cars.

It was all so ordinary. This part of the world was not, she thought, intended to be a setting for blackmail and murder.

And yet . . . As soon as she was clear of Main Street, Betty stepped on the gas pedal. She had to find Eve. It was her responsibility, and all the more so because she hadn't been firm about asking her about Denise's murder at their first meeting at the produce stand and then later when she'd seen Eve in the supermarket parking lot.

CHAPTER 22

WHAT SHE found at Zig-Zag was not what she had expected.

The parking lot held several cars, almost like an ordinary workday. She could not believe that George Hammond and Jerry Preston had reversed their decision about closing Zig-Zag, but here was some kind of proof to the contrary.

She parked and walked toward the building. The blinds were still lowered, but as she got closer to the door, she could see dim figures behind the glass.

Betty tried to door. It was open. She walked into the reception area to find Eileen, Marsha, and Tanya gathered at the receptionist's desk under the watchful eye of Mr. Caruso.

"Hi, Betty," Eileen said. "You're late." Eileen wasn't her usual perky self. She had two loaded shopping bags at her feet. They looked to be filled with her magazines and a couple of sweaters. She took a few objects from a drawer in the receptionist's desk and dropped them into one of the bags.

"Late?" Betty made a quick adjustment. "I'm sorry. I had business elsewhere."

Mr. Caruso said, "Mrs. Preston told the girls to be here at four on the dot to pick up their personal belongings."

"She opened up the place for us," Marsha said. She looked as though tears were not far away. "Mr. Caruso is here to see if there are any problems."

"And to be sure we don't take anything we shouldn't," Tanya said.

"Now, girls. That's not true." Mr. Caruso looked affronted. "I was asked to represent management so there wouldn't be any problems later. What with the murder here and the police."

"But why not Jerry to represent Zig-Zag? Or Mrs. Preston herself?" Betty asked. The Prestons seemed always to be just beyond her grasp and she had some questions for them.

"Mrs. Preston left," Tanya said. "She drove away without saying good-bye or sorry or anything."

"She took off fast by the back road," Marsha said.

"I'm done," Eileen said as she closed the last drawer of her desk. "She wasn't real nice to us, you know."

"She never was, and I never did anything," Tanya said. "They're all treating us like suspects or something."

"Surely not," Betty said. "No one said they were suspects, did they, Mr. Caruso?"

He shrugged. "I don't know anything," he said. "Why don't you just pick up whatever you left behind?"

Tanya said, "She didn't have anything here. She was only here two days."

Apparently Betty's good work on accounts receivable hadn't given Tanya any special fondness for her.

"Then let's get moving," Mr. Caruso said. "I got to see a guy about a job."

They began to shift toward the door.

"I couldn't believe it when Mrs. Preston called me last night and said she and Mr. Hammond were shutting the place down. I'm out of a job. I don't think they should be able to do that." Marsha was definitely going to start crying.

"Well, they did it," Tanya said. "Come on, let's get out of here."

"I told you girls there was a chance the new owners would take you on again," Mr. Caruso said. "I'm not waiting for that to happen, but maybe *you* should."

"A chance isn't good enough for me," Eileen said. "I

have to pay for this great wedding gown I found. It costs a fortune."

"New owners?" Betty said. "It's been settled? Mr. Mitsui?"

"I don't know about that," Mr. Caruso said. "I haven't talked to Jerry or George."

"Weren't you all here last night?" Betty asked. "I understood . . ."

"They were here for a while, but they left me to pack up some things," Mr. Caruso said. "We didn't discuss the business. Or the murders. I said something and they jumped on me."

"And Jerry's not here now? I understood—"

"Mrs. Preston came alone," Marsha said.

"Perhaps he's in the programmers' room."

"Nobody here but us," Eileen said. "And Reuben. He went to pick up his stuff in the copier room. Here he is."

Reuben sauntered in, a couple of denim shirts over his arm and a couple of screwdrivers in one hand. "These are mine," he said defiantly. "They came from home."

"Yes, yes," Mr. Caruso said impatiently. "Nobody's accusing you of stealing screwdrivers. If everybody's got what they came for, let's go." He started to herd them toward the front door.

They gathered outside as Mr. Caruso locked the door behind them. The key Betty had received from Reuben was still safely in her handbag. If he wasn't going to mention it, neither would she.

"I'm outta here," Reuben said. "You girls better start looking at getting unemployment."

"Good-bye, girls, Reuben. Good luck." Mr. Caruso made a move toward his car.

"Wait," Betty said. "Did anyone see a young girl around here today? Long brown hair, probably wearing jeans?"

"Here? Not me," Reuben said.

The others shook their heads.

Reuben and Mr. Caruso crossed the parking lot together

and drove away in their cars. The female staff of Zig-Zag seemed reluctant to leave.

"I wonder what Mr. Caruso is going to do," Eileen said. "He's kinda old to start a new job."

"He's not old," Tanya said, "and besides, he's got something lined up. You know salesmen can sell anything. Reuben will go work with his brother at the garage. What about us?"

"Yes," Betty said. "That's been worrying me."

The three young woman stared at her.

"What's it to you?" Tanya asked.

"I know there are reasons why a company has to close suddenly, but it doesn't seem right to put everyone here out of work just like that. It seemed like a good company and the new software would have made it even more successful."

"What do they care?" Tanya said. "Mrs. Preston's set with a rich father, and they'll probably get richer if they sell out. Jerry's just going to go off and play with his computers."

"It's all Denise's fault," Eileen said. "I said it when she brought that Japanese man here to meet Jerry. Remember I told you, Marsha? I didn't trust him one bit. And she was always looking out for herself."

"I remember," Marsha said. "But Denise promised . . ." She stopped.

"Yeah, what did your pal Denise say?" Tanya was sarcastic.

"Yes, tell us," Betty said. She wanted the three of them to leave so she could get back into the building without them seeing her, but she was curious about what Denise had promised.

"She said we'd never have to worry about our jobs. When she was running things here, we'd all be part of it. Now look. I got to find another job if Mike will let me. We need the extra check to pay for a tutor for my son."

"Well, I need a job, too," Tanya said, "but I'm not going to stand around and cry about it. I got kids at home who need to eat. Soon as I heard from Mrs. Preston last night, I started looking. I got an interview tomorrow morning."

"I wonder how much unemployment I can get," Eileen said. "Billy will know. Hey, Tanya. Call me sometime." Tanya waved as she walked toward her car, but she didn't promise to call.

"She won't call," Eileen said. "But you'll come to my wedding, won't you, Marsha?"

"Sure," Marsha said. "Mike won't, but I will."

"See you, Betty," Eileen said.

Betty watched the last of the Zig-Zag employees depart. Eileen seemed to be describing the wedding dress of her dreams, which she was going to have a hard time paying for.

Betty waited in front of Zig-Zag Incorporated, pretending to search for something in her handbag, until the two girls had driven away.

So Denise had been certain that she would be in charge of the company. Amanda had been certain she would sit in Denise's chair as the personal assistant to the president. It wasn't likely that Amanda thought that person would be Denise.

Someone had prevented both women from achieving their corporate goals.

When the cars had disappeared around the bend of the road in front of Zig-Zag, Betty took Reuben's key from her bag and unlocked the door again. Mr. Caruso had turned off the overhead lights when they left and the blinds were lowered over the plate-glass windows, so the reception area existed in a sort of half-light from the autumn sun, which was now low in the sky.

She stood beside the reception desk and planned how she would search the floor, office by office. She was certain that Eve had come here even if no one had seen her. She must have arrived before the office staff. She might even be hiding on the grounds somewhere, waiting for the opportunity to get close to the building when no one was around.

Of course, Betty's car was in the parking lot, but if Eve had seen Betty, she surely wouldn't be afraid to join her.

For a moment Betty relaxed. It was probably all a fool's errand she'd come on. Eve might be on the run, but perhaps she was not in immediate danger after all.

Suddenly she froze.

One of the lights on the telephone console came on. Someone was making a call from somewhere in the Zig-Zag building.

CHAPTER 23

BETTY STARED at the light on the telephone console. The first thing to do, she supposed, was to investigate the offices on this floor before descending to the programmers' lair down below.

Cautiously she walked along the corridor that led to the accounting room and the copier room at the end of the hall. Some doors were open, but no lights were on. She listened at the doors of the offices that she remembered were apparently unused but could not hear the voice of anyone speaking on the phone. She opened each of them carefully, but they were all dark and empty.

Back in the reception area she looked down the corridor that led to the offices of Jerry and Denise and finally to the locked door to the programmers' entrance. All of the doors were closed.

Instead of investigating each room on this corridor, she went directly to the programmers' door at the end and used Reuben's key. Just as the ponytail and plaid shirt microchip twins had told her, the key opened the door. She set the deadbolt to keep it from closing completely.

Now she had two escape routes: through the front door or down the stairs. Only then did she start to listen at the doors along this corridor. There was no sound from the conference room. She pushed open the door and found it empty. She checked the other offices on her way to Jerry's. It, too, was dark and empty, as was Denise's. She made her way across Jerry's office and switched on a desk lamp in Denise's room. It was still disordered and dusty from the police investigation, and the plants on the table in front of the window were beginning to look limp and sad. They hadn't been watered for several days.

This was not, however, the moment to be soft-hearted about plants. Indeed, even at her best, Betty was not especially gifted with growing things.

Since the person telephoning was clearly not on this floor, that left the storerooms and programmers' room downstairs.

She stood at the door of Jerry's darkened office, where only a stream of light from the lamp in Denise's office brightened one side of the room.

Out of the corner of her eye, she saw the light on Jerry's desk telephone go out. Betty thought quickly. She couldn't simply march down the stairs and confront whoever was there. Her only safe escape then would be a retreat back up the stairs. On the other hand, there was another way in.

Betty walked quickly back through the reception area and out the front door. She stayed close to the building as she headed along the side of the service road behind Zig-Zag, down toward the back door.

The remarkably peaceful view of the rolling, landscaped hills dotted with pines and laurels was a distinct contrast to the mild agitation she was beginning to feel. In the distance she could see the roofs of other buildings in the office park, where there were probably people bending over their desks, waiting for the end of the workday. That wasn't far off now. They'd get into their cars and head home for dinner and the evening news on television. Zig-Zag seemed remote from that ordinary world of business and domesticity and simple pleasures.

Betty tried the back door. It was locked, as she had expected, but once again Reuben's key worked. She pushed open the door carefully. The cement-block corridor was unlighted, and it became darker still when she closed the door behind her, making sure, however, that she set this deadbolt, too, so that it did not lock.

As she stood in the darkness, she knew what she was

doing was entirely foolhardy. She should have notified the police to handle this. She had left that message for Ted, but she had no way of knowing when he would return home.

If she didn't get out of this business safely, the state trooper's disappointment in her would know no bounds. Indeed, if things didn't go right, she would never get home again.

That had always been her problem. Betty Trenka believed that she could handle everything personally, but maybe this time she was wrong.

A fine time to come to that conclusion, she thought, but it's too late to turn around and leave. Eve might be somewhere in the building, and she had to find her. She had to find out who had been telephoning.

Although she had made it clear to everyone who would listen that she was coming here, it would be worse than foolhardy to announce her presence by simply turning on the lights, even if she could locate the switch. The only light at all came from a red bulb presumably over an exit sign at the end of the hall at the foot of the stairs. Not an ideal emergency exit if the programmers normally kept it locked to prevent bothersome women from invading their turf.

Her eyes began to grow accustomed to the dark, and she was able to differentiate between the pale cement-block walls and the darker frames of the doors.

She had her pocket flashlight, but it seemed to her that the best plan was to feel her way in the dark along the hall on one side trying the doors. When she reached the stairs, she would come back along the other side. That way she always had an available exit ahead of her. Somewhere along the way, of course, she would encounter the person who had been telephoning.

She tested her nerves. They were quite steady. She took a deep breath and felt a tingle of anticipation. She had no idea retirement would carry this kind of potential danger. She'd had her moments tinged with mild panic: the day the IRS came to audit Edwards & Son; the long-ago day she'd decided that the life she was living was damaging her and she would strike out on her own; that time she was a passenger in a car she knew was going to crash . . .

Somehow, those moments didn't quite match this one, where an ordinary woman with certain principles and a personal history that seldom deviated from forthrightness and honesty was sooner or later to confront someone who had turned so many lives upside down and ended two completely.

She started down the right-hand side of the corridor, the side opposite to the room where she had met the programmers. She pushed down on the levers of the first two doors she came to. They opened easily and revealed storage rooms, with walls of metal shelving loaded with fat looseleaf books, probably software documentation.

The third door was locked when she tried it. Then she leaned close to the door. She thought she had heard a sound inside, perhaps a muffled sob.

"Eve?" she whispered. "It's Betty Trenka."

There was no response.

Betty knocked very softly once, twice, paused, once, twice again. If someone was actually in the room, she—or he, for that matter—might recognize the knocks as a signal. She tried the signal again, then whispered, "It's Betty."

Now she did hear a sound behind the door.

"Eve?" Betty risked speaking a little louder.

The sound she heard was almost a sob and then the word, "Yes."

"I'm here to help," Betty said quickly, "but . . ."

She heard a sound down the hall and turned. The door to the programmers' room was slightly ajar, sending a sliver of light into the corridor, but no one appeared.

Here was another problem for Betty. She now knew where the person who had been telephoning was, but if Betty decided on an immediate confrontation, it meant leaving Eve locked in the room where she stood.

The building key was still in her hand, a mere dark spot on the palm of her hand. It was worth a try. She inserted the key into the odd-shaped keyhole like the ones on the front and back doors and turned it. She heard a click and almost laughed. Reuben's "mister key" was in fact the master key that opened every door at Zig-Zag. No wonder you needed written permission to have one made.

She opened the door quickly and stepped into blackness. She closed the door behind her and fumbled for the little flashlight.

"I'm sorry . . ." Eve's voice came out of the darkness.

"Hush," Betty said impatiently. "It's Betty Trenka."

Eve whimpered.

Betty found the flashlight and turned it on. This room was also lined with shelving filled with notebooks. At one side was a small copying machine and a table and a chair.

Eve was huddled on the floor next to the table. Betty was startled to see that she was wearing a familiar-looking blue flannel shirt. The sleeves were rolled up and the shirt was several sizes too large for Eve. It looked very much like Betty's favorite Saturday shirt. Eve had borrowed more than a couple of frozen dinners from her.

"I . . . I didn't mean anything," Eve said.

"Please be quiet," Betty said in a whisper. "I haven't saved you yet. We have to get out of this room and into another before we can talk. We don't want to be discovered."

She went to the door and listened. Then she turned out her flashlight and opened the door a crack. The door to the programmers' room was still slightly ajar. They would have to be careful.

"Stand up and give me your hand," Betty said. "Just follow me. We're going to go out of this room to the left and then into the one next to it. Do you understand?"

"Yes," Eve whispered.

"Come on," Betty said. "Don't make a sound."

She opened the door and pulled Eve after her and into the unlocked room. She shut the door behind them and then breathed a sigh of temporary relief.

"This is, like, the worse thing ever," Eve started to say.

"Not yet," Betty said. She was thinking about their situation.

Whoever Eve had seen at the site of Denise's murder, whether Betty's own suspicions were right or not, she imagined that an array of sharp lawyers would put the child on the witness stand and harangue and terrorize her, creating doubt about her testimony, proving she was simply a little blackmailer who had seen a chance to get money to escape from a life she disliked. With the doubt they would create, there was a chance that the murderer might go free, unless there was some other proof. A sensible, older woman who had also been in peril . . .

"Listen to me," Betty said. "Can you drive?"

"I got my license last year. My father only lets me drive once in a while. Usually he takes me places and picks me up. He doesn't trust me. . . ."

"I do understand," Betty said impatiently, "but we'll talk about that when we're clear of this business. I'm going to give you the keys to my car, a Buick. It's parked in the lot in front of the building. It's the only one there. Drive to Hammond Center and telephone the resident state trooper's office in East Moulton."

"I don't have any money," Eve said. "They promised—"

"I'll give you money. Tell them to come to Zig-Zag at once. After you call them, come back to Zig-Zag but stay in the car, away from the building."

"Okay," Eve said. "But how do I get out of here?"

"You're going to go down the hall to the left and out the back door."

"Yeah, that's how I got in. It was open."

"Someone locked it again, but I unlocked it. Run up the service road to the parking lot and then hurry." Betty put her hands on Eve's shoulders. "Promise you'll do what I say. Promise you won't try to run away."

Eve nodded. Her hair was disheveled, and her face was dirty and tearstained.

"No," Betty said firmly. "A nod isn't good enough. I

need to hear you say it. This is a dangerous business you've gotten yourself into, and me, too."

"I promise," Eve said. "Really. Cross my heart."

"All right," Betty said. "I'll see if the coast is clear. And please answer this before you go. Who summoned you here? Who did you see?"

CHAPTER 24

BETTY SIGHED when she heard Eve's explanation. It sounded like a bit more than she'd bargained for.

Then Eve was gone. She heard a very faint sound from her post at the half-open door, which probably meant that Eve had left the building.

I am too old for this sort of affair, Betty thought, but I will see it through, even though my new career path may be halted abruptly.

She had to count on Eve getting to the Hammond Center mall and making the telephone call. With the best of intentions, however, no one could reach Zig-Zag in less than half an hour. She could manage to wait that out, but not here in case Eve's captor decided to come looking for Eve in the locked room. It seemed to her that the best plan was to take the stairs up to the main floor, lock the programmers' door behind her to delay any pursuit, then wait there until it was time to summon the person for a confrontation.

She already knew how she would do that and where.

Betty opened the door and peered down the hallway. It was still dark. Although she had to pass the door of the programmers' room to reach the stairs, only she knew the door at the top was unlocked. She withdrew into the room and looked at her watch with her flashlight. Eve had been gone only ten minutes, barely time to reach Hammond Center and place a call. If Betty reached the upper floor, there were plenty of telephones, but the light on the multiline phone sets would tell the person on this floor that she was in the building.

She took a deep breath and went out into the hall, walking quietly but as quickly as she could. As she passed the door of the programmers' room, she heard an angry voice in a one-sided conversation, anxious words poured into a telephone receiver. Perhaps she only imagined that she heard panic in the voice. Panic was dangerous. Then she heard the receiver slammed down and the creak of the old wooden desk chair. Thankful for her old blue sneakers, Betty sprinted toward the stairs. She'd never been built to run like a gazelle, but she made it halfway up the stairs and beyond the dim glow of the red exit sign before the door of the programmers' room opened wider and a broad band of light fell on the floor.

She waited, holding her breath, but no one emerged from the room. Slowly, step by step, Betty moved upward. She felt for the handle of the door, opened it, and stepped into the familiar corridor of Zig-Zag. She could see the reception area ahead and beyond it the front door. If the worst happened, she could escape into the twilight—unless someone was coming in through the main door.

She locked the programmers' door behind her.

Her heart was pounding now. At least her doctor had repeatedly reassured her that her heart was in good shape ("for a woman your age," he always added), so she hoped it would not give out under the strain of the moment.

She walked carefully toward the reception area. No one was there. Her car was gone from the parking lot. She tried not to imagine Eve at the wheel of her car racing headlong to freedom in a distant city now that she had failed with her blackmail plan.

Oh, well. She could always arrange to get another car, although she didn't think her insurance company would be willing to contribute.

Betty found the list of intercom extensions at the receptionist's desk and carried it to Denise Legrand's office. She sat behind the desk. It was, she imagined, exactly where Amanda Glyn had been sitting when she died. She looked at her watch again. Twenty minutes since Eve had left.

If she was going to act, it would have to be soon.

"Zack/Peter, Prog 104." She thought she had found the extension number she was looking for.

And she had to stop looking at her watch. Twenty-three minutes since Eve had left. Timing was going to be very important.

Once more Betty was on her own as she lifted the receiver of the phone on Denise Legrand's desk, depressed the intercom button, and dialed 104.

She heard it ring. Once, twice.

"Who is this? Who's calling me?"

"It's Elizabeth Trenka, Nicole. I'm waiting for you upstairs."

"Where are you?"

"In Denise's office. Right where Amanda was sitting."

"I don't have to talk to you. I don't know what you're doing here."

"I know what happened, Nicole," Betty said, "and I want to discuss it with you." She thought she was beginning to sound like a stern supervisor who had caught a junior secretary dipping into the petty cash.

"You don't know anything." Nicole sounded contemptuous.

"Come upstairs."

"You can't order me . . ." Nicole stopped. There was silence on the line and then she hung up. Almost immediately, a light on the phone showed that she was calling someone. It took perhaps ten seconds. Then the intercom rang on Denise's phone. Betty picked it up.

"What do you think you know?" Nicole asked.

"Denise . . ." Betty began.

"That woman. She was taking the company away from us. Something had to be done. I understood that. She was going to be president, can you imagine? A slut from East Moulton kicking my husband out. She actually called me to gloat. Said she'd have everything. She even said that she and Alan . . ." Nicole stopped. "I told her my father wouldn't allow it and she laughed."

"And Amanda?"

"Another slut. She knew what Denise was up to with Mitsui. She claimed she knew what had happened to Denise."

"Somebody did know about that. I know what Eve saw that night. Friday night, when Denise was killed."

"Who'd believe Evelyn? Anyhow, she's out of your reach."

"No, Nicole. She's out of yours."

When Nicole again slammed down the receiver, Betty suspected she would take the time to look into the room where she'd left Eve. What her next move would be when she found Eve gone was definitely in doubt. After she looked into that room, it was quite possible that she would decide to take her car, which was presumably parked in the unused shipping room, and make her escape.

But where could she go? Back to the big new house on Oriole Crescent as though nothing had happened?

It was now twenty-five minutes since Eve had departed. Betty checked to see that the door from Denise's office into the corridor was not locked. Then she sat behind Denise's desk and watched Jerry's office.

Betty felt calm, surprisingly so under the circumstances. She wondered if she ought to find something to defend herself with, but again it seemed pointless. She would have to take her chances.

The phone started to ring somewhere in the building. Betty couldn't hear it, but she saw the light flashing on Denise's phone. She didn't dare answer it in case someone walked through the door, but she hoped if it was a person Eve had managed to reach, her failure to answer might encourage him or her to come swiftly to Zig-Zag. It might be too late, but at least it was nice to know that someone had bothered to show up to look for her.

After many rings, the phone stopped. Since Nicole hadn't answered it either, she must have departed after making sure that Eve really was gone.

The waiting was turning out to be the worst part of this

whole business. Betty was a person who liked to get things done now, tie up the loose ends, get on with things.

Suddenly the lights in the corridor outside Jerry's office came on. She could see an elongated rectangle of light on the floor of the adjoining office and then the shadow of a person entering the room.

Death at the hands of a possibly unbalanced, and certainly morally bereft, person was not what Betty had planned for her retirement, but it was too late to think about that now.

George Hammond stood in the doorway of Denise's office, backlit by the corridor lights. He looked very large, and even in the weak lighting he was purple with rage.

"You damned women," he roared. "You keep popping up like . . . like toadstools."

Betty stood up as he started for her.

"Don't be silly," she said. She was nearly as tall as he, and probably somewhat fitter, but scarcely a match for his bulk. However, he didn't appear to be carrying a weapon, although he'd managed to improvise successfully on two previous occasions. "You shouldn't have involved your daughter in the mess you've gotten yourself into."

"After the Cursey kid ran out on me at Denise's house and I couldn't find . . ." He stopped. "I had to tell Nicole, so she could get that kid over here. She recognized me from baby-sitting with Kathy. Nicole promised her a lot of money so she'd go away and shut up. She's downstairs now, and Nicole is back home like nothing happened. I'll handle Evelyn."

"Something did happen, Mr. Hammond. Eve is gone. She took my car and went to Hammond Center to call the police."

He relaxed a little. "Then the witness is gone. She'll keep driving until she hits the Pacific."

"Maybe not," Betty said. "You can't risk it, and now you have to do something about me. I've told people I was coming to Zig-Zag. The girls and Mr. Caruso saw me here earlier. I think things are closing in."

Hammond considered his plight. "How did you know it was me?"

"I thought first of Nicole—her jealousy, the rumors about Amanda and Jerry, Denise and Alan. Then I realized that this must be an office matter. Women in the business world who decide they are the equals of men like you and start making demands are seen as dangerous. In your case, that meant Denise and her deal with Mr. Mitsui. Then there was Amanda, another dangerous woman—for you. She appears to have known something about Denise's dealings and her death. I caught several hints of blackmail. 'Everyone wants money from us,' your daughter said. Amanda also wanted to be like Denise, leveraging herself up into an important job as she saw it on the basis of what she thought she knew."

Hammond was listening. Betty thought she had also been slipped into the category of "dangerous woman." She should probably hold her tongue, but talking meant delaying whatever he had in mind.

She said, "Denise had probably already handed over the new software to Mr. Mitsui, perhaps along with the source code. The programmers were uneasy about that. You don't really have a product to negotiate with now. You killed too late."

"But you don't *know* anything."

"I know that when you arrived the day I found Amanda, you knew to take the trooper to the conference room, so you wouldn't be in the way of the crime squad men, although you claimed not to have known what was going on. Of course, Nicole could have told you after you sent her here to check to be sure Amanda was dead, but she might not have had time to report to you. And then there was my old boss at Edwards & Son."

Hammond frowned. "Who?"

"A man who always advised me to be wary of the man who wrote the checks, the one whose money was on the line. That's you."

"Come along with me," he said.

"Excuse me?"

"I'm not going to just let you walk out of here. We're going downstairs. Then I'll figure out how to get you out of here, one way or the other."

"Of course," Betty said. She started to move as though she was going to come around the desk. She wondered if he really believed she would be so easily persuaded to descend to temporary or permanent incarceration in the basement of Zig-Zag Incorporated and probable death at his hands.

Hammond started to back up toward the door into Jerry's office, gesturing to her to go with him. She watched for her chance and when she thought she saw it as he started to turn his back to her, assuming she'd obey his command, she made a dash for the door to the corridor.

Betty was again thankful for her trusty old sneakers, and the fact that George Hammond's arrogance didn't allow him to imagine she'd suddenly make a break for it.

Once in the corridor she ran straight for the front door and out into the twilight. Hammond was close on her heels but not yet close enough to catch her.

Hammond's car was parked outside, but there was no one to be seen. No blue and white police car with its siren screaming and its lights flashing. Eve had failed her, but she wasn't going to give up without a fight.

Betty Trenka took to her heels, down the drive toward the road to Hammond Center. She couldn't hear Hammond running behind her, but he was probably getting into his car to follow her. She judged that as soon as she heard his car, she would scramble up the gentle incline at the side of the road and remain out of his reach for the moment.

Then she did hear a car behind her. She was not accustomed to this sort of exertion and wondered how long she could keep it up. Obviously, if she got out of this situation, she was going to pay closer attention to her doctor's orders about exercise.

Betty had her eye on a curve up ahead. If she could make it around that, she'd be out of Hammond's view for a brief moment and could escape to the grounds off the roadway.

As she rounded the curve, she saw in the distance the low beams of a car's headlights coming toward her from the direction of Hammond Center.

She couldn't tell if it was her car with Eve behind the wheel. It certainly didn't look like the police. It was so indistinct in the twilight, and she decided she couldn't risk stopping it in case Nicole was returning. Even if it was Eve or the police, they would see Hammond's car driving away, and when they reached Zig-Zag, they'd discover she was gone from the place.

She looked back for a second. Hammond's pursuing car was very close behind her.

Then she nearly fainted with relief.

Mr. Mitsui's limousine glided to a stop at the opposite side of the road.

The uniformed driver hopped out and opened the back door, as Hammond's car almost braked in front of her and then sped away into the oncoming night.

"Madam?" the driver said, and indicated that she should enter.

"Thank you so much," Betty said as grandly as was possible with labored breath and a pounding heart.

CHAPTER 25

"THE POLICE are blocking the road at the entrance to the office park," Ted Kelso said as Betty sank into the luxuriously comfortable seat of the limo. "We got there just ahead of them. I think the car that just passed won't get by."

Mr. Mitsui said, "Good evening, Miss Trenka. I am most concerned that you are well. Shall we find medical assistance for you?" He indicated the bar that took up the center of the wide backseat. "There is sherry here."

"No, no," Betty said, although she was completely winded. If she had been at home, a sherry would have been welcome. "It's nothing. How do you all happen to be here?"

"Eve called Penny after she called the police. Penny called me," Ted said. "I was just starting out to rescue you when Mr. Mitsui came by to pick you up for dinner. I commandeered him, and we joined forces."

Mr. Mitsui bowed slightly.

"Limousines in East Moulton stand a better chance of breaking the speed limit," Ted said, "and besides, I am not sure that my wheelchair is any match for a murderer. Mr. Mitsui was able to telephone the police and finally convince our trooper that Eve was serious about your predicament here."

"Thank you so much," Betty said faintly, "both of you."

The driver proceeded to the driveway of Zig-Zag to turn the limo and head back to Hammond Center. Suddenly two police cars with the sirens and lights Betty had hoped for tore into the parking lot.

The disembodied voice of the limousine's chauffeur said, "I think they want us to wait."

"That's all right," Betty said. "They either got George Hammond now or they didn't."

"George?" Ted seemed surprised. He stroked his nicely trimmed gray beard and looked serious. "I was sure from what you'd said that it was Jerry because he was so obviously not a killer. George Hammond, eh?"

Mr. Mitsui made a small sound as though drawing in a sharp breath.

"It was simply a matter of business," Betty said, "and George Hammond couldn't handle the changing times." She looked at Mr. Mitsui sternly. "I think you have not behaved well in this," she said, "but I will assume that Denise Legrand assured you that it was acceptable behavior to receive the software program she promised you. Perhaps even delivered to you."

"It is not quite so simple," Mr. Mitsui said. He did look a little guilty. "She claimed to have the right to do so and said that Mr. Preston had agreed to sign the necessary documents. Then Mr. Hammond assured me that although he was the principal investor in Zig-Zag, the business was in the hands of Mr. Preston and Miss Legrand. This morning, however, the picture changed. I am," he said proudly, "an honorable man."

"Yes, well . . ." Betty began, but their state trooper was rapping on the smoked-glass window. It was magically lowered without apparent human intervention.

"I'm terribly sorry about all this," Betty said to the trooper.

"You are unharmed?" he asked. "Good. I'm going to have to have a long talk with you, Miss Trenka. Are these gentlemen taking you home?"

"Yes, I suppose so. I'm afraid Eve Cursey has absconded with my car. And after she promised she'd come back."

"She hasn't taken off with it," the trooper said. "We told

her to stay in Hammond Center. We like to keep things as uncomplicated as possible." He looked pained. "This probably won't affect our case and may even help it."

"I'll testify," Betty said. "George Hammond admitted to me . . . These gentlemen will confirm . . ." She looked at Ted, who shrugged, then at Mr. Mitsui, who looked, for want of a better word, inscrutable. "Do you have other evidence?" she asked.

"I really can't comment," the trooper said. "But trust me, we're handling things."

Not another one who handles things personally, Betty thought. "Do keep an eye on Nicole Preston. She's devoted to her father. She doesn't kill people apparently, but George Hammond's little girl is what we used to call a chip off the old block."

"Mmm. Can I find you at home in the morning? About eight-thirty?"

"Certainly, Officer," Betty said. "I'm out of work."

Mr. Mitsui again made his small sound of indrawn breath. The trooper started away toward the front door of Zig-Zag.

"Wait," Betty called after him. "The front door is open, but perhaps you'll need the key." He came back. "It's a master key, opens every door in the place."

"Does it, indeed?" said the trooper. "Amazing."

"I suggest," Ted said as the trooper walked away, "that we leave now, so we can get Elizabeth home early. She has to be rested and refreshed for her interview tomorrow with the authorities."

"That is an excellent idea," Mr. Mitsui said. "We will dine and then take Miss Trenka home."

"I couldn't," Betty said. "I'm not dressed." She felt extremely grubby and disordered.

"We will go to a place I have enjoyed in the past," Mr. Mitsui said. "The matter of dress is not important."

"Not Mom's Luncheonette."

Mr. Mitsui actually smiled broadly. "Pork chops. Grits. Black-eyed peas. Sweet potato pie. Very American."

"Southern and Soul?" Betty said. "That place in the big white Victorian house?"

"Actually very good," Ted said. "And it's no problem for me getting in."

Mr. Mitsui was still smiling. "We will discuss your future work with my organization. I understand now that you are wiser than I first imagined."

Ted leaned back in his seat as the limo sped away. "A career option you can't refuse, Elizabeth?"

"I think," Elizabeth Anne Trenka said, as she considered whether she had sufficient hairpins in her bag to make her hair at least look decent, "I think that I am retired. I am looking into beekeeping."

Mr. Mitsui kept smiling.